Bataille's Wound

Bataille's Wound

Michael Greene

STATION HILL ARTS
BARRYTOWN, LTD.

Published by Barrytown, Ltd., Barrytown, New York 12507 for Station
Hill Arts, a project of the Institute for Publishing Arts, Inc., a not-for-
profit tax-exempt organization in Barrytown, New York.

Grateful acknowledgement is due to The National Endowment for the
Arts, a Federal Agency in Washington, D.C., and to the New York State
Council on the Arts for partial financial support of this project.

Distributed by Consortium Book Sales & Distribution, Inc.
1045 Westgate Drive, Saint Paul, Minnesota 55114-1065.

Cover Photograph by Susan Quasha.
Typesetting by Alison Wilkes.

Library of Congress Cataloging-in-Publication Data

Greene, Michael, 1954-
  Bataille's wound / by Michael Greene.
  p. cm.
  ISBN 1-886449-04-X
  1. Bataille, Georges, 1897-1962—Fiction. 2. Authors,
French—20th century—Fiction. I. Title.
PS3557.R386B38 1995
813'.54—dc20   95-2810
                                                CIP

Contents

increscunt animi, virescit volnere virtus

Note on citations from Bataille

I have left the titles in French. The translations are my own. All references are to the twelve volumes of the Gallimard edition of Bataille's *Oeuvres Complètes*. The volume number of the citations are noted first in Roman numerals, followed by the page numbers.

Hammers, Files, Dynamite

I am in quest of a vital intensity indistinguishable from intoxication. I want more energy than I need; I want to overflow. Therefore, I have a limited use for words; and do not restrict myself to them. Words subordinate more often than they invigorate. I experience them as beneath me, and I make no effort to live down to them. When they cease to intensify me, I jettison them. By this rejection, I attempt a transformation from a slave to a free spirit, from something useful to something noble, from something definable to something incomprehensible.

I want to be a sovereign being, a life that loves to be alive, a flame that takes delight in burning; and, so, I take delight in destroying whatever would constrain delight, for in doing so, I burn all the brighter. What I would like to accomplish is something akin to a jailbreak. What I collect here is nothing meaningful, just some wedges and files, a few hammers, and perhaps an occasional explosive charge, useful tools for getting outside the order of utility, and, for when the work becomes too tedious, some random recreation in the form of fireworks and jokes.

☙

My thoughts and desires grow out of Bataille's as grass grows out of loam, as life leaps out of death. In writing this, I celebrate him, lingering over his inky remains, devouring his corpse to intensify my own vital charge. When I write in the first person, this should not be taken as something other than Bataille's thought, for I am able to say something akin to what Catherine said of Heathcliff, what Bataille himself wrote of Nietzsche, and what Nietzsche wrote of every name in history: I am Bataille. And being Bataille, I am also Nietzsche, also every name in history; and, so, history is over, and it is necessary to begin again. A passionate question breaks out like a flame, and one must either decisively burn or pursue an extinguished form of life.

The Axe Blow

This is not an argument, it is a question, or, rather, I am a question, one that frightens me. The key is not something logically demonstrable, but something lived. I am not harmonious with the universe. I am perplexed, anxious, beside myself, writing. I am a trembling of the world. If I were to be harmonious, I would be no longer; someday I will be harmonious, and that is why I am anxious. Anxiety is my chance. I am a fear of dying, a fear that this is it, and if I were to lose this fear....

I want this fear; that is, I want to be. Besides, whatever frightens intensifies. Fear is more valuable — more desirable — than truth, and so I search for fear, I search for what I am.

> What am I afraid of?
> I am afraid of time.
> I am afraid this is it.
> **This is it.**

Anguish is the *a priori* that makes decision possible. Anguish puts everything at stake and leaves it all to chance. If I were to give reasons for my anguish, I would avoid my anguish, which is my depth, an abyss devoid of reason.

My absolute: my despair.

This is it, decision is everything. Decision, being without basis, appears miraculous. If it takes a divine being to create such an event, then I am a god; but I am so only by decisively going beyond myself, which in any case *feels* divine.

To be inner experience is not to remain attentive to ideals. Ideals get in the way. If I see myself in terms of ideals, I consider myself as something known from the outside, and so I deny my immediate experience; I dodge *my immediate and obvious confusion*. The ideal sets up a hierarchy, a pyramid, which, once accepted, situates me, determines me as something graspable, measurable, divisible into pieces.

2

A totality of existence is not a collection of capacities and accomplishments. It no more lets itself be cut into pieces than does a living body. Life is the virile unity of the elements that constitute it. There is in it the simplicity of an axe blow. (I, 529)

I am a living body. I am how it feels to be a body. I am inner experience. Does anyone expect me to obey that which mutilates me?

When I decide, the decisive current of the universe, the entire universe, courses through me. My outbreak — my decision — like any volcano, involves the cumulative pressure of the globe and the empty draw of the sky.

Without the night, no one would have to decide, but, in a false light, submit. Decision is that which is born before the worst and overcomes. It is the essence of courage, of heart, of being itself. And it is the inverse of project (it wants one to renounce delay, decide at once, risk everything: the consequence is a secondary concern.) (V, 39)

> To decide. To risk. To err.
> My life: my error.

The need to decide, the experience of the night, indicates a dreadful and sovereign existence. Since calculation is only a tool, it is incapable of being sovereign — decisive. However this has never stopped humans from shifting the responsibility of their judgements (their values) onto the edifices of Reason, Philosophy and Theology. An individual or a group condemns another individual or group, perhaps to death, but instead of admitting that it is their decision, they evoke a metaphysical apparatus, a handy god, of whom they claim to be only the spokesmen and instruments. Whoever opposes their feigned absolutes is met with their condemnation. By deferring responsibility for their judgement, they diffuse their sovereignty; they become hollow masks.

You will only escape by braving what you fear. (IV, 192)

In this absence of absolutes, in this river, time, it is still possible to decide, not as an emissary of an absolute, but as a sovereign, anxious being.

Usually when people say, "act responsibly," what they mean is: "cow-tow to the comforting lies that we call truths." The insertion of a metaphysical claim into an argument attempts to create two illusions: the universal validity of the claim and the ability of the speaker to make metaphysical decrees. The grandeur implied in the second deception is undermined by the subjugation implied by the first, for an individual acquires the right to speak metaphysically only by forgoing his or her own authority, becoming the servant of an ideal. Only a willing slave chooses to abandon his or her authority, and a slave who wills to be a slave is a slave indeed.

 C3

A willing slave gets upset if you refuse to acknowledge his or her master.

C3 8O

I refuse the timid trickery of claiming that God told me what to do, and I also will not pretend that my decision is something akin to the solution of a technical problem. I will not follow a manual, and I will not take orders. I will not consider a human sacrifice to be an abstract and passionless event.

Language and Time

To speak, to think, short of fooling around or of..., is to rob oneself of existence: it is not to be dying but to be dead. It is to go into the extinguished and calm world where we habitually drag along: there everything is suspended, life is deferred until too late, from deferral to deferral... The small time lapse of projects suffices, the flame goes out, the tempest of the passions is followed by a calm. (V, 59- 60)

All language, whether philosophical, theological or scientific has a limited range; words, even used perversely, are still too charged with the familiar. Even when cursing the inadequacy of words, they are still words, and, no matter which ones they are, they fall short. Surpassing and overwhelming words is silence, not an empty passivity, but that which destroys the efficacy of words. Extreme experience wrecks language. Silence tears language apart.

 C03 80

Ineffable. — Silence is linked to extreme interrogation; and language is a flight from silence, a flight from that which is overwhelmingly perplexing.

Slur — Language demeans and degrades the unique, the tangible, the silent, and the lost.

Common language. — Words keep chattering away as if everything is common, as if everything can be repeated, everything known, but everything is extraordinary, happening instantaneously, fluttering in a single breath.

C03 80

Ostrich wisdom. — When frightened, an ostrich buries its head in the sand; and in a similar condition, a human being may bury its head in words. We can do things with words, use them in a sovereign manner; but we can also hide beneath them and avoid ourselves.

Word trap. — It is easy to become a word addict. Words always lead to other words, and so once you get started, it is easy to get caught; like an animal in a snare, the more you try to get away, the more you become entrapped.

Short leash. — The experience of the night is rare because men are as faithful to language as dogs are to overbearing masters. In philosophy this currish fidelity is expressed whenever language is given an ontological status.

Although words drain us almost completely of life — of this life, there is almost not a sprig that has not been seized, dragged, accumulated, thronged together without respite, by these bustling ants (words) — , there subsists in us a silent, hidden, unseizable part. (V, 27)

And not just a part — it is me, my heart of hearts. Anything I or others can say of me can only obscure this.

That which counts is my vital distaste, distaste for what I have been able to say, write, which could bind me. (V, 45)

C3 8D

When words are seen beneath, I experience something strange and familiar — something words typically avoid; but if I attempt to direct words toward it, they always fail. Even poetry fails. (It must fail).

The word 'mystical' is too comprehensible; the word 'silence' makes too much noise.

The drowning silence from a cadaver's mouth, which renders words useless and mute, is the shibboleth to this realm.

C3 8D

Scripture lesson:

Do you expect someone who can write to worship ink? Ink is dead. Words dead. How can I help but notice that?

I do not depend on Hermes. I do not reverence Troth.

My name is something about me, but it is not me; indeed even the word *me* is not me. *Me* makes too much sense; it obscures the confusion which wrecks me. If the word *me* worked, I would be like some other me. This I refuse, refusing the word *I* as well. Words — put simply — do not reach. They are, at times, like emanations, solar rays, something other than the sun. My pen, which is not me, secretes ink.

Heraclitian Wisdom

Somme Athéologique. — What holds Bataille's works together is the persistence of that which tears them apart — time. Bataille's work marks time, and time differs from itself. It is the drive of the oldest psychology, causing opposites to spring from opposites, making things come together and fall apart.

The violence that tears at Bataille's thought is not a singular violence, not a specific thing. This violence is violence itself — the movement that carries things toward the abyss, by which beings become beings and then become nothing. Attempting to express this movement, he renders an image:

I mark down an image describing (rather badly) an ecstatic vision: "an angel appears in the sky: it is only a brilliant point, having the thickness and the opacity of night. It has the beauty of an inner light, but, in an incomprehensible wavering, the angel raises up a crystal sword that shatters." This angel is "the movement of worlds," but I cannot love it as if it was like other beings. It is the wound, or the crack, which, hidden, transforms a being into "a crystal that shatters." (V, 258)

Experienced as divine, initiated by an angel, this movement is inconceivably profound *"having the thickness and opacity of night."* (V, 258) The sword is lifted up and against the abysmal sky, like an obelisk, a declaration of power; and at its height, like a wave at its crest, it falls to pieces. The movement of the angel, the movement that lifts the crystal sword (the crystalline fragility of things) to its place of sacrifice, is named the *"movement of worlds;"* it is the boundless and complex current that bears off and dissolves all things. It is the shock of dawn and the fall of night. Ungraspable, it defies conceptual thought. It is time itself, not as a container or a dialectical progression, but as Cronus, the inscrutable trickster, butcher of his father and devourer of his children, but also, strangely, a phoenix rising from an egg of ash. It is that which Bataille expressed when he wrote: *"time signifies only the flight of objects which seemed real."* (V, 89)

To feel the pervasive draw of the creative and destructive movement of time is to swim in a tragic current. To appreciate it is to acquire an awareness for tragic beauty, the beauty of withered flowers, and rotted fruit. How delicate everything is: all in time, all the victim of time.

New wave. — Think about something immediate: the organic material you are. Do you think this is the first time it was alive? The stuff you are, your flesh, before existing as your flesh, was that of other mammals, fish, birds, insects, flowers, fruit, and before that still others and others. You are not the first time this water has been a wave. What a delicate potion you are, what a strange and exquisite concoction.

Heraclitian wisdom. — Nothing abides. In time the pyramids will erode; the last grain of sand will tumble and become lost in an abysmal desert floor. My ancestors, winding through time, who, what, where are they? And what will become of me? The earth or sky will open up like the jaws of a predator, and I will be lost. When the time comes I will be nothing; nowhere; and before, or after, or with me, everyone I have ever loved will be lost. This is the movement of worlds. When things reach their peak, they are at the place from which they fall. The hilltop is a place of sacrifice. Even when things seem still, they are quietly shimmering, expending themselves.

I am and you are, in the vast flux of things, only a stopping point ready to gush away. Do not delay in achieving a precise awareness of this agonizing position: if you happen to cling to stuffy goals within limits, where no one is at stake but yourself, your life will be that of most people, it will be "deprived of the marvelous." Stop a brief moment: the complex, the gentle, the violent movement of worlds will make of your death a splashing froth. The glories, the marvels of your life, were due to the surging of the wave which bound you to the immense noise of a downpouring sky. (V, 112)

CB EO

Standing over a Grave Heraclitus Speaks:

At the extremes, there is nothing that is not time, and time is something else.

To say that being is time is to be without center or stability, each moment mocked by the next, whatever is becoming foolish.

9

Time is like an acephalic man, destroying and creating by fits, without purpose, something to be enjoyed, a laughable monster.

Time, like a child playing, poses obstacles to itself. If time is taken seriously, whatever is laughable is grave, and whatever is grave is laughable. All authority is unstable; indeed instability itself character-izes ebullient power. Time itself is power, a play of forces, destructive and creative at once.

Authority no longer belongs to God, but to time whose sovereign exuberance puts kings to death. (I, 471)

C3 Œ

To say that being is time is to say that the copula must copulate again and again. *"Gold, water, the equator, or crime can indifferently be announced as the principle of things."* (I, 81)

Due to the fundamental lack of stability of being — and of the word being — anything can serve as a center, a church chime, an idea, a particular shade of blue; but the energy builds as tedium grows until suddenly a tangential burst sends attention — and words — rushing toward yet another center which in turn is destined to have yet another vertiginous consequence.

C3 Œ

Aristotelian time: Even when linear seeming to curve, rotating around some center, known or not yet known, but knowable, perhaps even to itself. The thoughts in a rational person's head can serve as a basis of time, a ring dance around judicious principles; like Plato's vision of time in his *Timaeus*, time circulates around what is not time, around what cannot be threatened by time.

But all sovereignty is linked to time, and, so, what can withstand the sovereignty of time?

Bataille also writes of circular motion, going so far as to describe it as basic, but this movement is no longer around a fixed and abiding center, but one that is itself mobile. Furthermore circular movement is itself complemented by yet another movement, linear and tangential. Circular movement can spin off with a disruptive ecstatic energy, an energy that at its peak can only lose itself in a vertiginous gyre around an indeterminate absence of abiding, so thoroughly lost that one can no longer distinguish between curve and tangent, tangent and curve, each escaping itself, lost in the failure of itself and its other.

A circle is a mockery of a line, and a line, of a curve, unleashing a laughter that reveals the parody and vulnerability of each to each. Anything will do as a center, but only for a while, and only to become laughable and lost in laughter.

And if the origin is not akin to the ground of the planet seeming to be the base, but to the circular movement the planet describes around a mobile center, a car, a clock, or a sewing machine can equally be accepted as the generating principle. (I, 81-82)

An indeterminate number of combinations writhe around the various forms of the verb *to be*.

ᘒ

A drunk dancing in traffic. — The origin of things (which is continually present as absent) is a whirling dervish of incomprehension. The only reason we think that there is something other than time is because we ourselves are so thoroughly and briefly time, that we are lost, passed over by time, before we have enough time to see that everything passes, nothing abides, everything is time. Having but a moment, we look at things such as animals, each assigned a place by words, and because we do not abide, we do not see that the taxonomy was but an occurrence, like anything else, a rare event at a rare time. Life is not stable, and even less constant is what we say about it. Over time, animal species, including our own, rise and fall, and with us, whatever we say. Words are waves as delicate and evanescent as winds over sand, establishing patterns that in time become lost.

> pyramids crumble
> continents part
> mountains erode

seas weep
stars explode

Whatever exists is time, a movement that devours itself and recreates itself out of its own corpse, but only as something to be devoured.

Because **time is**, everything becomes nothing. Time thought concretely is tragedy. Time: the breaker of bonds and the object of sudden horror.

Time being time, being insubordinate, does not move with constant regularity: occasionally, time explodes — cadavers, eroticism, catastrophe, lightning; but on other occasions, time is so gently violent, the delicate hush of his last breath.

At the core of fact is fiction, idiotic narratives: subject, verb, object. X did Y to Z. I think a thought. The lover loves the beloved. We find a scapegoat at the cost of having a feeling for what occurs.

Causal thinking uses blunt mechanical categories which pretend to make events comprehensible, overlooking slippage — the transformation of events — which can be experienced only as incomprehensible. There is no such thing as cause and effect, only slippage.

Philosophers extol the rigor of logical thought, and others, the rigor of architectural forms, but that which is most rigorous, the inexorable movement, time, dismantles all other pretensions of rigor. The rigor of time, which eats away at one's body with the insatiable insistence of vultures devouring Prometheus' liver, is a dreadful violence. Nothing is more horrible; all other horrors derive intensity from it. The rigor of time is unsettling, and encountering it, most people seem driven to avoid it; and so they sneak away from their exquisite chance.

But sometimes, someone has the strength not to turn away and gives heed to it, and finds himself or herself suddenly changed. This movement transforms its vulnerable devotee into a voluptuous being, thoroughly intimate with time, indistinguishable from it. One is a being composed of time, washed in time, like a river tenderly and violently devoured by a sea. No longer a being with concise limits, no longer enduring, one becomes a vertiginous flow, a shimmering risk, a lucid ecstasy on the verge of night. To devote oneself to experience — to time — is to become a body, and nothing but a body, a sun kindled to flame by night.

Bataille's Optics

My father smacks me and I see the sun. (II, 10)

I have naked buttocks and a bloody stomach. Very blinding memory, like the sun viewed red, through closed eyes. I imagine my father himself, being blind, also sees the sun in blinding red. (II, 10)

My father, blind, desperate, and yet, his wasted eyes toward the sun. (V, 335)

CB EO

The universe is at once day and night.
Our sun is in the middle of a nocturnal abyss.
Its light is squandered in darkness.

Light itself blindly seeks an absence of light.
I too am a sun.

CB EO

The star at the center of our solar system has a diameter that is one hundred and nine times that of the earth. More than its size, its intensity makes it stunning. At times it emits tongues of flame over two hundred thousand miles long (approximately the distance from the earth to the moon). At its center, the temperature is fifteen billion degrees Kelvin. It incessantly destroys itself, losing 4.6 million tons of mass each second. While it is, in a very direct manner, ultimately responsible for all the various dynamic, climatic, and biological movements of energy on the surface of the earth, the sun's outflow is not dedicated to these earthly effects. The vast majority of the sun's energy is thrown into empty space. In excess of 99.999 percent of the sun's expended energy hits no planet whatsoever. In human terms it is wasted, a pageant of destruction.

The sun is an ecstatic object, not a placid orb; it is a circular sea, flaring more intense than tangential, releasing perpendicular rays, wasteful beams, the image of a madman slashing himself, spurting blood, losing himself in an insane movement beyond himself.

The earth and its atmosphere are sensitive to the sun. In this regard, the earth is like a giant unattached eyeball. We live at a mean distance of 92.9 million miles from the sun, receiving a mere one two-billionth of its radiation, and yet despite the magnitude of this distance and the paucity of this portion, if on a clear day you were to fix your gaze on the sun, it would almost immediately bring you to tears, and within seconds begin to burn a hole in your optic nerve. Although the sun is frequently used as a symbol of the rational order, a rational person would not dare look at it. A rational person maintains a lucid vision by averting his or her gaze away from the source of vision.

Our rational thought does not begin with the discovery of firm foundations, it begins with a flight, an attempt to dodge that which fills us with terror and threatens to overwhelm us. The search for foundations occurs long after the flight is underway; it is an attempt to avoid what terrifies.

Bataille recounts the following event, supposedly recorded in Michelet's secret diary:

"In the course of his work, it happened that he lacked inspiration: then he would leave his house, and make himself enter a public convenience where the smell was suffocating. He breathed deeply and, in this manner being "drawn close as he could to the object of his horror," he would return to his work. (IX, 220)

We are all like Michelet: we get a good whiff of our ruin and that sets us reeling, running toward reason. Once we are far enough from terror, we say something like, "I am going to work."

Rationality usually entails carefully and clearly scrutinizing things, but there are certain things which reason avoids. Indeed, it looks away from life's basic movement; and so it cannot affirm what it does not acknowledge. (But glory is only possible if life is affirmed.) Such a conceptual system is not just blind to the blinding aspects of the sun; it is blind to all the blinding aspects of experience. If you attend to life, and if you are willing to endure the burning tears such attention requires — tears of laughter, love, and loss — then you may find that the deepest experiences are so dazzling as to be blinding. But that hardly renders them insignificant; unless by insignificant one means that from which one must flee out of terror.

ை

Plato gives the sun a privileged role in the allegory of the cave, using it as the symbol of the regularity and sublimity of the ideal, but a reasonable person only contemplates the sun, avoiding the pain a direct encounter would entail. In a similar way, paying attention to an ideal world involves ignoring time. This life, however, is nothing but time; and like the sun it must expend itself.

ை

The flight of Icarus. — At the pinnacle of Daedalus' technical and conceptual achievement lies the occasion of his son's destruction. Daedalus stands amid water into which his son has fallen from an ideal height, and his eyes break into tears, which fall and are lost in tomb-cool waters, from which his son is no longer distinct.

Just as there are things at which a rational person does not look, so too there are things a rational person is forbidden to take seriously. These are generally given a marginal status, considered as nonsense, useless, insane, vulgar, etc. Rational thinking avoids that which it fears and, when it can, it considers the terrible to be trivial; but that which it fears is real and, ultimately, cannot be avoided. If there is to be exuberance in the meantime, our time, the fearsome must be confronted, defied.

ை ைை

Rather than a rational foundation, Bataille's work suggests something else: a crucial relation between reason and unreason.

ை ைை

"Night too is a sun." — Zarathustra

Rational thinking looks down on the unknown as a mere lack of knowledge; its image is an empty and passive head. Such an image does not do justice to the experience of the night. A more faithful image is a burning bush, or even better, a head struck by lightning, ablaze, with eyes dazzled and vacant, mouth howling, stammering, or barely breathing, but still somehow alive.

At the extremes of experience, there is nonsense. Knowledge usually ignores nonsense, but at the extremes, its capacity to ignore is devastated. Nonsense is the explosion of what previously had sense. It exposes the folly of calculation; it leaves articulation mute. Rather than being a privation, *"there is a fulguration, even an 'apotheosis' of nonsense."* (V, 55)

The limits are obliterated, and there is a vertiginous fusion of undeniable force. The experience of the unknown is moral, intellectual, and aesthetic, but all at once, indistinguishably voluptuous. As everything rushes together, only the distinction between things is lost. The abyss is not the empty lack the mundane order considers it to be. The experience of the night is potent, a lethal threat; indeed it is the potency behind every lethal threat. This night is not just a want of daylight, its darkness bears its own extraordinary, fearsome inner light. It is impossible to describe, not because there is nothing to describe, but because its onset overwhelms our capacity for description like the sun overwhelms our gaze. The sun burns and blinds the optic nerves, the night dazzles and pierces the heart.

I try to write about it but it deflects me, casts me gleaming, no more than a ray.

ભ ฒ

The sun's plunge into darkness is its glory. Our dead sun, earth, feeds on the living sun.

ભ ฒ

I want to have the simplicity of the sun.

಄ ಄

Pseudo-Dionysos. — Of course I have a blind spot; I am alive. There is a blind spot in sense, and this blind spot is not, as one might suspect, something trivial and secondary. It is the ground, the absent ground, of significance. Negative theology approaches that which rational thought tries to dodge, that which is obvious at the extremes.

Rivers Into Seas

At the highest height there is depth; at the apex of sense, nonsense.

The summit of the intellect is at the same instant its exhaustion, its swoon.
(III, 151)

Setting out, accept nothing as true unless it be indubitable. I do not find what Descartes found. He did not question enough. The *cogito* is not the residue of a process of unlimited questioning. On the contrary, it represents that which Descartes was unwilling to call into question — grammar, the self, and the primacy of reflection.

A standard summary of Descartes is that he doubted revelation, sought to take nothing on faith — a covert agent infiltrating and undermining dogmatic authority. In fact he only transferred the authority of religion to reason. Instead of getting rid of revelation, he set down new revelations, expressed a new faith, the dogmas of modernity. The authority he denies scripture, he transfers to semantics; but his thought — the thought of the modern world — is no less pretentious than positive theology when it comes to making claims about the identity of the universe and everything in it.

Contrary to Descartes' prescriptions, at the extremes of questioning, I am not certain of anything. I lack the means to put an end to my questioning. My rigor drives me mad; compels me toward an abyss. Extreme doubt cannot be articulated. Words fail.

When I write *I*, I do not mean a *cogito*, but an incarnate question. My residue is a deaf, mute infant in a dark chamber. Astonished.

 C3 8O

I write about Descartes, it could just as well be Hegel or any other philosopher. Hegel's revelation: the absolute whispering in his ear and for his ear — "The rational is the real and the real the rational. Amen."

The greatest intelligence is at bottom the most duped: to think that one has apprehended the truth when one only avoids, vainly, the obvious foolishness of everyone. And nobody really has what each one thinks: something more. The puerile belief of the most rigorous in their talisman. (III, 151)

We all have what so many make such an effort to avoid — the naivete of children.

Life is going to lose itself in death, rivers in the sea, and the known in the unknown. Knowledge is the approach of the unknown. Non-sense is the issue of each possible sense. (V, 119)

The frail truth: The truth of doubt, the evidence of immediate, un-bounded confusion.

CR

Erroneous truths. — Truth is the outer veil of the impossibility of truth.

Unknown saints. — Whoever ardently seeks the truth (accepting nothing dubitable as true) ends up mouthing the words of a saint: "Oh Unknown Nothingness."

Divine nonsense. — The divine is the pinnacle of sense, but the pinnacle of sense is the destruction of sense.

Discordant concord. — Inner experience has a community and tradition, but Bataille, in a spirit of decision, breaks from this tradition and community as a way, paradoxically, of giving unprecedented authority to what is at the core of the community and tradition. He belongs to a community, made possible by Nietzsche, that knows it will be betrayed and is bound by a feeling of complicity in this betrayal.

Nothing to keep us apart. — At the extreme, there is no difference between the authority, the method and the community of experience. Experience is ecstasy, which is itself the need for communication. There is a refusal of anything that would keep things in place; the limits are breached, ecstatically dissolved, opening onto radiant nothing.

The end of experience? — What is at stake in experience is not an intellectual adventure with a discontinuous destination, rather a ceaseless search in which one can only be lost and then lost utterly.

Although there are communities that give witness to it, the question is not initiated by any tradition or scholarly enterprise; rather the question is life in the face of death.

Religion and theology. — There is a fundamental and irreconcilable difference between religious experience and positive theology. Theology provides answers to fundamental questions; religious experience, in contrast, entails being racked by crucial questions and experiencing a devastating absence of reply. Religious experience requires going to the extremes of supplication, something theology precludes.

Reciprocal. — The more theological, the less divine.

Absent intensity. — There is something divine about the absence of God when this absence overwhelms.

The limits of reason. — In order to be rational, it is not a question of regarding everything in a rational manner; it is question of paying no heed to things that breach rationality, of ignoring whatever leaves us stammering or mute.

Insignificant questions. — The question that I am, you are, cannot be answered or even consoled by philosophy or theology; indeed, more often than not it is ignored, regarded as insignificant.

The delusion of articulation. — Those who are most articulate, those who can clearly discern and disseminate their position, are those who are most eloquently and preposterously deluded.

The failure of comprehension. — Conceptual thought is incapable of conceiving how utterly astonishing everything is. In this it lags behind art.

Abysmal lucidity. — "(What like a bullet can undeceive!)" Herman Melville, "Shiloh"

Understanding at the extremes. — When a human heart is torn, knowledge becomes useless. One may still grasp, but in vane. One's hand gropes and closes into an empty fist, still gripping, clenching, until its strength gives out, until the pain and exhaustion open one's fist like a flower, grasping nothing.

Extremely perceptive. — Everything appears in and against the abyss.

Streaming. — Humans come into existence as such frail and watery things, and after a while they die and are but memories. In time, those memories and those who had those memories are lost. Life's exuberant streaming outstrips itself.

Holy ground. — The states which Bataille terms delight (or glory) are godlike, godlike in the sense that one decomposes as one approaches them.

Pathos of distance. — The abyss is not just deep; it is incomprehensibly high, so high and deep that one loses the distinction between the two. Like Nietzsche in *Ecce Homo,* one is ascending and descending at once.

Familiar unknown. — For a long time I sought to discover the meaning of existence. There were times I actually thought I had arrived at my goal, but I always came back to the same condition, that of not knowing. My search had the effect of overlooking something obvious. I was trying to avoid an unavoidable terror that had been there all along, the absence of meaning, the boundless horizon for all the feeble things I did know. Face to face with it, I was flooded with a familiar despair. This unknown, this night, my soil and lack of ground....

Out at sea....

The All-Knowing?

Death of comprehension. — The death of God was necessary in order to restore the sacred, which was on the verge of being eclipsed by the comprehensible.

Divine knowledge? — Is God really imagined to know something, to know everything, as knowledgeable as a room full of Hegelians? Philosophers, obsessed with the project of articulating the mind of God, imagine such a deity, with nothing better to do than to consider knowledge. (He is talking to himself again). Their god is an impoverished being — not very godlike at all. If one feels divine one has no need for knowledge. Knowledge is what characterizes a useful thing, not a divine being.

God imagined as someone who knows everything, incapable of being amazed, smug and uninspired, answering every observation with "of course." Such an existence would be so boring he might slit his wrists, or butcher his son. If god was really attentive, he would not be able to believe in himself. He would not know anything. Language would crackle and burn: "Why am I God?"

We are idiots not only when we are perplexed but also when we pretend everything makes sense, when we surmise the questions are stupid. But what could be more foolish than a blind fool pretending not to be one? But to have questions, to burn with them? That too is foolish, my experience. Discontented with the familiar, even the liminal, I do not want to be content; to be content is to sleep. I stay up and become lost in the night, divinely absent.

ॐ

Decisive darkness. — The preface of *Zarathustra*, to say nothing of the teaching of eternal return, can be read as a vision born out of a mystical experience. In it, Zarathustra comes out of a long solitude, a solitude that is shared by animals; Zarathustra must have become an animal because he communicates with animals, feels with them, regards them

22

as friends. Next he goes down to humankind. This descent leads him to a vision of abysmal tragedy: a man on a tightrope, a man with a tenuous existence engaged in a dangerous activity. In short, he is alive. Walking a tightrope, surrounded by a lethal abyss — such is his life. Zarathustra witnesses the tightrope walker's fall. At the bottom of the abyss Zarathustra converses with the dying man, blesses his life and death. Then he carries the dead man into the woods were he passes a night in the presence of death, in the presence of absence. This night is decisive. Out of it, a sun emerges.

Ecstasy. — Ecstasy can be reached by challenging knowledge. Ecstasy itself cannot be defined. It involves the breaking of limits. It is not a state of higher knowledge, but overwhelming perplexity, an astonishing awareness of the impenetrable poetry of things and of the failure that is at the heart of poetry.

Fidelity to the quest for the divine opens onto absence. God? That is a word I use to invoke the night, but the night is not God. (It is not night.) It differs from itself. It rips everything apart.

Utility's Enigma

The discoveries of science are, at best, pragmatic inventions, often quite useful. Being useful, science should be our servant, and wherever it ceases to be so, it should be discarded. If a scientific truth ceases to serve and begins to devitalize, it has lost its value. Pure science is nothing but metaphysics, that is, an ascetic illusion.

Vitality, not utility, is the sovereign value. If we forget this we miss life itself. We may even fall into the trap of regarding the devitalizing as valuable. Instead of using utilitarian thought as a tool in the service of joy, we can impoverish ourselves, assigning ourselves a pragmatic (servile) significance.

Knowledge, the totality of our sciences, is surrounded inside and out by what we do not know. Perhaps our calculations will insure our destruction. Whatever we hold to be certain is in fact a crap-shoot, and we do not even know the odds.

Useful thought. — Calculative thought, the strategy of a rational mind, is guided by utility. However, if something is useful, for example, a hammer, it aims at something else. The value of the hammer is not the hammer itself but its result. As such, value is deferred, and if utility is the sole value, an endless deferral occurs: I do A in order to achieve B; I want B to get C and C to get D, and D, E, etc. Eventually what is needed is not a means but something valuable in itself, otherwise there is a problem. This problem is not the intellectual vacuum Aristotle abhors, it is how life would feel if it were reduced to utility.

The task is not to abandon calculative thought, but to subordinate it. Use it, and not be used by it! Use it to survive and intensify, not to be enslaved. Keep it beneath us; keep it from making life wholly profane. Life is primary. Work is secondary, and it should be in the service of vitality, in the service of high spirits.

Pragmatism is a useful way of regarding things, but it is not what the search for truth was after. Pragmatism is in a void.

I think? What am I? I encounter an aggressive absence. I have thrown away my philosophical amulets; my rigor gives out. The night becomes apparent as something I cannot see. It omits a dark ray that pierces me and drains me.

You can still hope, even if you do not believe, but I am hopeless, or rather I want to be strong enough not to need hope. I imagine those with hope to be consumed by hope, wasted by hope, but not like martyrs at the stake, not dying but as if dead, left for dead, bored, sedated by hope.

The experience of the night should not be confused with skepticism. Skepticism is a method of producing knowledge, using doubt to refine information; the night, however, is not a means. It does not purify knowledge; it wrecks knowledge and the ability to know.

That which I do and think in order to survive is not what I am. I want an excess beyond survival. I want delight. I want to subordinate calculative thoughts and actions to an ecstatic intensity.

I am a being too uncertain to serve as a philosophical foundation; this anxious metaphysical impoverishment that I am is my sovereignty: it is the possibility of my decision.

Cʒ ȣɔ

Chance: the most potent name for night.

Calculation attempts to eliminate chance. One plans against it, math-ematically examines the possibilities, figures the odds. But probability equations do not express chance; they express formal regularities, and these themselves are threatened by chance. When a plan succeeds, chance can be disregarded; but when at its limits, calculation fails, chance appears, more inescapable than prison, more penetrating than a vulture's beak. Chance is bound to appear as something you did not or could not plan against. Chance appears like the night, with the night, inextricably linked. Like the night, chance is experienced as being abysmal, incomprehensibly unbounded.

Night is a richer representation than being. Chance comes out of the night, it returns to the night, it is the daughter and mother of night. Night is not, neither is chance. Chance being that which is not, reduces being to a deposition of chance (a chance, which withdrawn from play, searches for substance). Being is, according to Hegel, the most impoverished notion. But chance, according to me, is the richest. Chance is that by which being goes to ruin in the beyond of being. (V, 326-327)

Night is richer as a representation than being, because being comes out of night, and will be lost in it. To become aware of the night — the unknown — is to become aware of chance. If you ask the metaphysical question — why is there anything at all? — and you experience the absence of an answer, then things appear to have no ground; they just are. This experience of things being without ground is the experience of them being by chance.

I will take my chance; it is my only chance.

Blue of Noon

Le Bleu du Ciel is about what can happen out of the blue.

Out of the blue, a letter arrives, a train arrives, a plane arrives, a man is shot dead, a woman goes crazy, an impossible love occurs, bombs drop, people plot to liberate prisoners, Nazi youth play music — and a man and a woman fall into a grave as if into a starry sky.

ᯣ ᯤ

Conceptual thought forbids an experience of things.

ᯣ ᯤ

Wild position. — Nietzsche's tightrope walker, dangerously alive, leading an existence out in the blue, and out of the blue he meets his fate. Others look up to him, but they do not have a feel for him. They avoid how it feels to live without ground; this in spite of the fact that they — everyone, you, I — are over, under, and surrounded on all sides by an abyss.

ᯣ ᯤ

No matter how one tries to avoid an awareness of tragedy, it is impossible. In the midst of a felicitous day, with a friend, on a beach, splendid weather, perfect water, an idyllic moment — there is happiness. However, in the midst of such felicity, perhaps because of it, there twists an inexorable violence.

At that moment that which cruelly rises up in him, is comparable to a bird of prey which cuts the throat of a smaller bird in the midst of an apparently peaceful and clear blue sky. It seems that he will not be able to carry out his life without giving in to an inexorable movement, the violence of which he can feel exerting itself on his heart of hearts with a rigor which terrifies him.
(I, 552)

His heart suddenly plummets toward an awareness of tragedy, for the thought comes: "This moment is exceptional. This moment is but a moment. It will pass — it is already passing." And so the exuberance gives birth to the tragic realization that it is impossible to continue. Even if life was constituted by a continuous stream of such moments, life itself, being moments, must pass away. An awareness of existence's fleeting rarity can make joy painful.

CR

By fleeing an individual does not escape suffering; he or she merely alters it. Such a one no longer faces despair, but remains agitated, empty and false, shunning the grief of the dying only to become passionless, dead — not delirious, but sober to the point of morbidity.

CR

The sun at its zenith is an incomprehensible event.

CR ED

Late at night, almost dawn, agitated and aggressively awake from thinking about Bataille, in a last ditch effort to fall asleep I start drinking beer and reading mathematics. The math text, full of catchy examples and illustrations, is not at all difficult. I am no mathematician. One example, in a chapter on statistics, makes me break into a fit of laughter which dissolves any hope of repose: the number of possible combinations of human DNA molecules is 10 to the 2,400,000,000th power — an overwhelmingly large number, considering the estimated number of atomic particles in the entire universe is a comparatively small 10 to the 76th power. What I find absurd is that I, against all

28

odds, am one of these combinations, and so, statistically speaking, my odds of being me are 1 in 10 to the 2,400,000,000th power. Of course this number would have to multiplied by the inconceivable odds that there is anything like DNA in the first place or, for that matter, that there is anything at all. To put it simply, I am an unlikely event. Nonetheless, somehow, I am.

I am, and, what is more, I demand to be, not only in spite of the ocean of improbability out of which I emerge, but in front of the other sea towards which I stream. Stating this, I realize how ridiculous I am, but I decline to take back my words. I prefer being laughable to being nothing. Besides, what drives me is not logic, certainly not mathematics, but something to which reason is necessarily blind, a groundless and futile compulsion; it is what I am, my idiotic, even insane depths — my instinctive body, my gratuitous exigency, my animal impulse to exist.

ᘓ ᘔ

Nietzsche wrote that he often took solace in the thought of suicide; I never understood his remark until I read Bataille. (Bataille exhibits the depths, "the swamps," of Nietzsche's thought.) The solace Nietzsche found in the thought of suicide is that of one who approaches death only to find how much he loves life. Things that intimate death — sexuality and terror — have the ability to evoke the shocking awareness that I am and fervently desire to be.

This impulse that urges me to be, that refuses not to be, is what makes me anxious before the void, unable to calmly glide toward it as I do toward sleep. From the perspective of this insistence, there is a difference between sleep and death: sleep appears as no threat, even as a sustaining comfort; whereas death appears as the threat of all threats, the ultimate and unbearable menace. The failure to recognize this difference, to feel it, is at the core of Socrates' last arguments and renders them unreal and unconvincing. Even if the arguments are intellectually rigorous, they are incapable of changing the way I feel, and, at bottomless bottom, that is what I am. A being is not how it is conceptualized, not how it is known from the outside. Naked existence experienced most intimately, from the inside, is how it feels to be. Life is not eidetic; it is dramatic.

ങ ജ

If you were to ask me what I am, I might dodge the question, describe myself as others see me, as an identity or job; but at the extremes, I am only how I feel, how it feels to be alive. Narrow definitions and purposes stripped away, a dramatic being remains, comic or tragic, delighted or desperate, a healthy or unhealthy insistence.

ങ ജ

There are dramatic flare-ups that ravage the linguistic edifices in which we hide from ourselves: the birth of a child, the death of a loved one, a disease, an attack, an erotic encounter. These events initiate an awareness of how it feels to be. There is also yet another unexpected way of dismantling these linguistic props: words — for example, Bataille's and Nietzsche's — have an uncanny ability to help us escape from words. Their texts are punctuated by word-crashing bursts of silence, which lead to a position from which words are beneath sense, at best good or bad servants of nonsense, the nonsensical and exuberant way it feels to be dangerously alive.

ങ ജ

Everyone dies, but no one is there for his or her own death. You cannot make it to your own wake, and your corpse, while capable of inspiring terror and disgust, will be incapable of affecting you. However, in a limited way, we can be aware of our impending death, and this awareness is a characteristic we use to distinguish ourselves from animals. A bird, a poet wrote, can freeze to death on a tree limb, but it will not be conscious of its approaching doom. It is odd that when we think of death, my death, your death, it has the effect of making us quite aware of our own fragile animal existence; it lets us experience ourselves as something other than that which we habitually interpret ourselves to be. Instead of a mind, a soul, or a human being, one discovers oneself to be agonizing flesh, a mysterious chord falling into silence. Nothing reasonable anymore. Deprived of a future, anticipation no longer possible, one is incapable of distancing himself from how he or she feels. Mortality — an intense encounter or intimation of it — has a voluptuous character. One feels intensely, and one feels it is impossible to continue. Impossible. Utterly impossible. Nonetheless, a defiant and deviant energy asserts itself, the exorbitant violence that one is. Like a lonely, transcendent god, over and against the universe, one cries out: "I demand to be. I refuse death." But, at the extremes this is an impossible desire. I am by turns a potent and an impotent refusal of death. My being is my potency, my ability to be, the raw fact that I am.

03 80

At the extremes, anguish is nothing heady. There is voluptuous terror. To experience it is to feel as frenetic as a wounded animal, desperately searching for a way out, a way of maintaining sovereign frenzy.

03 80

The experiences that are interpreted as "mystical experiences" are more widespread than the interpretation. It is not that experience is so rare; rather it is rarely taken seriously — except at the extremes, as it occurs.

During such experiences, it is impossible to know what is happening. One is racked with spasms of life, a child crying, each spasm setting the torch to that which previously appeared as sensible. As exhaustion nears, prior significance is once again glimpsed, but as if it were a delicate veil, under which writhes an inconceivable and vertiginous depth, the impossibility of knowing, the unknowable unknown. Unlike experiences of knowing, in which the object is kept separate from the subject, the limits that make things comprehensible are breached. I am unknowing lost and mingling with the unknown, no longer knowing what I am, no longer knowing.

31

I was a child left with a dying man
when he had died
I was a child
a child

to be a child is not to know
what a child is
I am a child
a child

a wheel that rolls out of itself
lost to itself
lost

a splattering of stars
against a starry sky

*Before god the mystic had the attitude of a <u>subject</u>. Whoever confronts
existence has the attitude of a <u>sovereign</u>. (V, 278)*

Inner experience concerns wild surges of vitality. In religious circles,
these overflowing states have been designated as mystical states, but
experience itself demands that such designations be challenged and
denied. Experience puts everything into question. Typically the word
mystical is used to link such states to a tradition — Judaic, Christian,
Buddhist, Islamic, etc. — and thus to an interpretation, a domestication
that imposes limits; whereas what occurs is without bounds.

Extreme experience is not logical thought, not conceptual servitude. It
is peak intensity.

 C8 80

Holy Sacrifice

Theology is the metaphysical pretensions of grammar given mythological garb. If theologians would have their way, their work would maintain the status of supreme knowledge. Accordingly, God himself, the preeminent utility, would be given several important jobs: creator, bedrock of salvation, metaphysical insurance man, guarantor of all righteous order. The supreme being may be regarded as logically necessary, but such a concept is foreign to one who experiences the divine in sacrifice, experiences the death of an other. The concept is incapable of consuming us, merely keeping us in line. If one is to experience the divine, it is necessary to sacrifice the God of reason. The death of God is the liberation of the sacred from the conceptual (the useful). It restores the freedom of divinity and the divinity of freedom.

If I would choose to serve God, I would not only reduce myself to servitude, I would reduce the divine to petty mastery. God, whether the commodity of the theologians or the sentimental construction of the pious, is too comprehensible. Either one gets in the way of an apprehension of the unknown. Poetry is preferable to both, but poetry too falls short. Although it introduces the strange, it does so my means of the familiar, and thus it keeps one foot on accustomed ground. The strange — the utterly amazing — is, like Eurydice, inaccessible. It is nothing poetic. Poetry is still beautiful, and beauty is a terror that disdains from destroying us, but at the extremes, we are destroyed. The extreme of beauty is not beautiful. It obliterates all form. Poetry is an approach. It is like a ladder kicked away once we reach the ledge, leaving us hanging, helpless. It is true that the poet finally does get past poetry, Orpheus finally mingles with Eurydice, but at the cost of his life. There he lacks the means to be poetic.

႙ ႘

For Bataille the dramatic is essential: *"It is simply to be."* (V, 24) Inner experience is felt, and if you lose your ability to feel, you lose your existence. Moreover, a diminution of feeling is a diminution of being. To appreciate what is at stake here, it is necessary to reject external means, particularly language. Language makes you regard yourself as if from the outside, as something graspable, possessing definite limits. It evades the dramatic given of your life; it conceals the openness of your incomprehensible existence. Describing yourself as this or that thing, obscures your most immediate reality. Rational language denies that we are time. Among words, poetry alone makes an attempt, an exquisite and hopeless attempt, to reveal the ungraspable and overwhelming fragility of our time, of our existence. Poetry has no object; it is in passionate accord with the fierce and frail shimmering of existence. It witnesses the blossoming of time, which blooms into silence.

Insubordinate Discourse. — While language is used to make the unfamiliar familiar, poetry, which introduces that which language habitually avoids, makes the familiar unfamiliar. Through a fulgent and dramatic sacrifice of words, it introduces what is not known, but felt, and felt in the uncanny way the unknown is felt.

ᏣᏍ ᏍᎧ

When I no longer dodge what I am, I do not know what I am. I am obscure inner movements.

I live by sensible experience, not by logical explanation. (V, 45)

ᏣᏍ ᏍᎧ

Instead of attending the unknown, religions have often allied themselves with the advance of knowledge. This is particularly obvious in the movement from myth to theology: positive theology is knowledge, and, as such, it does not concern itself with the unknown.

We have a tendency to think of ourselves as something definable but from one period of history to the next, from one culture to the next, the definitions change. Still, the task of assigning ourselves a linguistic identity continues. Bataille's thought contests this process, and it does so with dazzling evidence: inner experience. Furthermore, it is inner experience itself which impels him to this challenge. Inner experience is our existence stripped of purpose and interpretation.

ᏣᏍ ᏍᎧ

The Space of Death

That which occurs cannot be articulated. Words are no good. It is a hole punched in words, a gap that threatens to draw everything said into its insignificance. One must become incomprehensibly divine in order to die. Dying one enters an exhausting isolation. My death is for others, but my dying (living) is mine.

When the sun explodes such a glorious tragedy of the sun.

I am deflected.

CR

This infinite improbability from where I come is below me like a void: my presence, above this void, is like the exercise of a fragile power, as if this void demanded of me the defiance I myself bear toward it — myself, that is to say the painful infinite improbability of an irreplaceable being, which I am. (V, 84)

Anguish indicates a fear of being communication, of going beyond; it indicates the price and value of ecstasy, a loss of self.

It is in dying, without possibility of escape, that I will catch sight of the laceration that constitutes my nature. (V, 85)

Even when dying, I am alive. But I am not dead. Or if I am, I do not know it.

One must *live* experience. Experience tears me to shreds.

I think, I write, on account of not knowing any way to be better than in shreds. (V, 81)

The Loneliness of the Dying. — Lacking the strength to communicate, no longer able to get beyond, a sun collapsing, no possible way out.

Communication

Refutation of the problem of solipsism. — Watching some children play, I see one of them break away, running with abandon. She falls on the pavement striking her hands and knees. I do not feel the shock to my hands and knees, but my body feels the shock, the shock to my heart. Sometimes I feel the shock more intensely than the child. A person with a weak heart can die from the trauma of a loved one in danger.

Bound. — Because I am communication, I cannot separate myself from others, no more than I could separate the individual cells of my body. The health of the community, of humanity, of the surface of the earth is intrinsically mine: effect it and you effect me.

Being is wounded. — Communication is not known; it is felt. It requires not an intellect, but a wound.

Naked existence. — The dramatic is not an addition to existence; it is our existence. Everything else is evasion and dupery.

Shallow trap. — The pitfall of the dramatic: mistaking it for the melodramatic or sensational, which, in contrast, are comprehensible.

Decisive. — The dramatic is the impossibility of remaining indifferent.

Contra free will. — Decision is something other than free will; it is what is felt decisively. It is not a faculty; it is the outbreak of that which I am.

Burning authority. — The authority of experience is the authority of drama, the tragic force of sacrifice.

Minor spiritual exercises. — Listen to a conversation and forget about the information that is passed along; instead feel that which is communicated. Listen to it as if it were music — what is the tempo, tone, and intensity? What would it feel like to make such noises? Do the same

towards animals, winds, seas, heavy and light clouds, empty night skies.

A companion proof for the existence of God. — I cannot stand to be a groundless mortal; therefore, there must be a God.

Beyond me. — Drama is not simply what I feel, but how I feel when I am beside myself. I am beside myself.

Experience

The strangest is that non-knowledge has a sanction. (V, 65)

Those who become intimate with the night, who ally themselves with it, have the authority of the night. The experience gives them the right to call everything into question, but because it is the night that grants this, an expiation is required. You must die. Blanchot states, *"Experience itself is authority."* Then adds, *"(but that authority offers itself up)."* (V, 19)

The sun burns, but in burning loses itself. An individual has authority because he or she is, but such glory consumes itself.

Being is the place of sacrifice. Anything that is, because it is, can and must be sacrificed, must be drawn gently or furiously into the night. In spite of the fragility of our position, we are at a pinnacle, like the crest of a gratuitous wave. When the wave has reached its height, it may hover, but then the fall begins. Cresting is collapsing.

ങ ഓ

Experience is not a question for proofs. It must be lived. The question itself is evident. It opens onto and mingles with silence.

I am my desires. But I will burn of them, necessary flames.
My desperation — the sour fruit of my desire — is my necessity.

We are not everything — we have only two certainties in this world, this one and that of dying. (V, 10)

I know this because I feel it, a feeling that threatens not only my ability to know, but my ingenuity for existing. These two certainties are charged with doubt: certain uncertainties, my paradoxical being. No solutions; nothing is revealed.

There is night. I am lost, and it invigorates me to refuse to pretend I know where I am. I admit I do not know what I should be doing. For now this does not disappoint me; quite the contrary, I enjoy being afloat: all I want is the strength to be like a wandering star in an empty sky. I want the strength not to need reassurances and promises of salvation. I want to find delight in being as I am. In the Preface of *L'Expérience Intérieure*, Bataille recounts a desperate story of a quest for joy carried to extremes. Following Nietzsche's advice (which itself is laughable) not to accept anything as true unless it has made you laugh at least once, Bataille attempted an ontology of laughter. His analysis of laughter opened up unexpected regions; it seemed to him as if there were *"no more riddles to solve."* (V, 11)

He was filled with a feeling of triumph, sensing that he had solved all the great mysteries — laughter and reason, horror and light, even death became clear. Then, at this pinnacle, a new problem appeared.

I woke up before a new enigma, and this one, I immediately knew, was insoluble: this enigma was so bitter, it left me in an impotence so overpowering that I experienced it like God would experience it, if he exists. (V, 11)

The Torment

The torment is not the opposite of laughter, it is the extreme of laughter, the divinity of laughter. It is laughter going beyond, leaving one behind to die. It is the laughter of children heard from a dying woman's window when she no longer has the strength to laugh, when she feels that she will never laugh again. Divine tragedy. Wasting flesh.

I enter a blind alley. All possibilities are exhausted, the possible steals away and the impossible attends. To face up to the impossible — exorbitant, indubitable — when nothing is any more is in my eyes to have an experience of the divine; it is analogous to corporeal punishment. (V, 45)

God!

Like Bataille, I do not use this word like Descartes or a theologian. I cry out.

God?

The word __God__, to avail oneself of it in order to arrive at the depth of solitude, but to no longer know, hear his voice. To be unconscious of him. God, the last word, desiring to declare that all words, a little further on, fail: to attend to its own eloquence (it is not avoidable), to laugh until in an ignorant daze (laughter no longer has a need to laugh, nor sobbing to sob). Further on my head explodes: man is not contemplation (he has peace only by fleeing), he is supplication, war, agony, madness. (V, 49)

The summit of joy is despair, the awareness that joy cannot continue. At the extremes of despair, it is clear that one must die. It is a lack of strength that makes it desperate rather than joyous. If one had the energy, it would be delightful.

Every outburst of intensity is followed by exhaustion.

CR

I cannot resist becoming the divine absence to which I cry out; I become isolated and impotent, unable to preserve myself. I am all at once.

> I am the divine absence
> a son forsaken by his father
> a father slaughtering his son
> a spirit ablaze
>
> Alone I hear my plea for mercy
> I fail myself
>
> An incandescent hush halo and core
> I desert myself
>
> I am what the word God attains
> evaporating deity
>
> breathless lord fragile lord
> invalid god
> wasting flesh

I do not understand what I am; I feel what I am. I do not know what I feel.

Words do not overpower me: I spit them out. At extremes I find them useless.

CR

Joy is to be a burning bush, unconsumed. But to be ravaged by flame is despair.

The Exhausting Solitude of God

The temptation to be God, to take responsibility for everything, to achieve the *amor fati* that characterizes divine existence — that requires an unprecedented transgression. It is sinful to love the world as it is, to take joy in this eternal crisis, time.

> I am a sinner. I willed this world into being.
> I love things as they are.

ଔ ଓ

I am thinking of a sea dove
dying on a beach
no longer flying
collapsed in on itself
barely breathing
I imagine dying like that

Prayer

Standing, I appealed to that God who, in my heart, tore me to pieces, and whom that heart, breaking, could not restrain. It seemed to me in my agony that the void invaded me. I was too little, too wasted. I was not up to that which was overcoming me, to the horror. I heard the thunderbolt fall. (IV, 185)

There are moments one finds oneself in tears, on the floor or in a corner, utterly alone, supplicant.

> Bring me to the extreme
> an apathy toward every particular thing
> loving the vast expanse
> obliterating all distinctions
> erase the words good and evil
> wipe away pleasure and pain
>
> offend my taste and ruin me
> with delight in everything
> unbearable delight

Canticle in Darkness

Intonation: At the extremes
  eros and *agon*
  meet the same night
  the night of nights

Chorus: cold night
  dead night

  indeterminate chamber
  desert sand
  empty wind
  burning pyre
  butcher block
  holy altar

crushing hand
strangling grip
dissolving ring
absent lord
venereal wound
withered breast
living hell
extinguished flame

Like Job on a cold dung hill beneath a moonless sky.

Varanasi

At the extreme limit, you are guilty of all sins and all sins are forgiven.

At the extreme limit, there is dead silence, the sound of funeral pyres and flowing water.

At the extreme limit, there is a glimpse, perhaps of written words or a lover, but as if through water.

At the extreme limit, the glow of sandal wood powder over inflamed mango boughs, and then ashes, ashes lost in water.

Sacrifice of Words

In *La Somme Athéologique* there are prayers:

O Heavenly Father, You who, in a night of despair, crucified your son, who, in that night of slaughter, in accord with that agony, became **impossible** *— to the point of screaming out — you became the* **Impossible** *Yourself and experienced impossibility to the point of horror, God of despair, give me that heart, Your heart, which fails, which gives out and can no longer bear that you are!*
(V, 47-48)

God who sees my striving, give me the night of your blind eyes. (V, 53)

These prayers make sense of nothing; these words move relentlessly towards a breaking up. They exhaust themselves, hold nothing back, point toward no future; they are hopeless, the last words before waves of violent, unrelenting, engulfing silence.

ᴄꜱ ᴃ

> I am God but only as Christ
> abandoned in the Garden at Gethsemane
> or sailing on a mast
> beneath an abyss
> at Golgotha
>
> My heart is nowhere I feel it
>
> Oh Brilliant Black consuming my flesh
> Starless Night
> under and above me
> I said I was
> King of the Jews

Night Song: Supplication Without Response

In the Gospels, Jesus prays most ardently as it becomes clear that he has been forsaken. In the Garden of Gethsemane he sweats blood, and at Golgotha, laid bare to death, he pronounces the most desperate words: "lamma sabachtami."

In the midst of life, when it is still possible to preserve oneself, the *pater noster* is possible, but at the extremes, everything the *pater noster* asked for proves impossible. One is an abandoned orphan on the threshold of an infinite night. That which is crucial is not the words; the words fail. That which is momentous, although incomprehensible, is the silence that follows one's ardent request.

Cʒ ꙍ

In St. Ignacious' *Exercises,* the saint exhorts the devotees not to be content with knowing what is stated; they are called upon not simply to memorize or contemplate some doctrine of Christian belief, but to imagine the crucifixion and to feel its dramatic force. In a similar way, St. John of the Cross spurs the devotee to feel what Christ felt, the agony of a god dying, forsaken, betrayed, at the extreme of despair. He invokes us:

We ought to imitate in God (Jesus) the fall, the agony, the moment of "non-knowledge" of the "lamma sabachtani." (V, 61)

Bataille takes up the saints' challenge.

*One does not know in what manner one ought to speak of God. My despair is nothing, but that of God! I am not able to live or know anything, without imagining it lived, known by God. We back off from possible to possible, in us everything recommences and is never **gambled**, but in God: in the "leap" of being that He is, in his "once and for all"? Nobody would go to the end of supplication without putting himself in the exhausting solitude of God.* (V, 48)

Cʒ ꙍ

The imitation of Christ not as pious fraud but as dying man.

It is necessary to be a god in order die. (V, 86)

ᘓ

A godlike solitude and sovereignty. One is all at once, holding nothing back. But at the extremes there is exhausting solitude; there is no God, only the "lamma sabachtani" and the exhausting, utterly desperate silence that follows.

"Lamma Sabachtami"

Vain impudence of recriminations. (V, 53)

If like a god, whether Jehovah or Baal,
I would condemn whoever abandoned me,
I would only underscore my own impotence.

But I cannot resist the lament.
In the whimpering voice of a dying god,
I snivel, "How dare you desert me?"

It is a voice too weak
almost unspoken, unheard
marks in the swirling dust
nothing at all, nothing

The Mocking of Christ

You are no hermaphrodite Buddha
with flipper arms and
a flame coming out of your head

you do not have eyes
like memories of deserts or
lips like shadows in the night

You do not have lotus palms
You are not clothed in scrolls and emanations
There is no illuminating script on your back

You do not have elongated ears
so you cannot hear everything
you cannot hear me
and what if you did?
(my thought falls to pieces)

You have no knowing smile
You have no third eye of insight
You are as lost as me

Your ridiculous beard cannot hide you
Your swollen feet give you away
You are not God; you are a man!

Naked as can be with the bloodied knees
and stained flesh
of a dying man

pale divinity slightly jaundiced lord
your chest is drained of blood
it collects in your feet
it drips from your head

Your penis is like a dying bird frightened, ashamed, forgotten
nothing but itself now

exhausted, dull flesh of Jesus my parody and essence

stripped by a goon wearing an animal skin
gawked at by a cretin leaning on a spear
poked at by a genuflecting idiot's wand

let me love you become you

ash and pale flame
on a ground of mist
against a backdrop of night

Kyrie

oh desolate lord oh broken man
have mercy on me

a halo of stabbing thorns mingling blood and sweat
hands anointed with gashing iron
have mercy on me

man butchered on a wooden sail beneath an empty sky

give me strength let me feel what you feel
and live

let me know what the dying know
and live

my pen goes into the page
like a crucified man lost in the night

⦃ ⦂

Our whatever that art nowhere
Give us our daily sin and forgive us of guilt

There are times when an individual prays so fervently that he or she is
indistinguishable from god, that is, from god's absence. At such
moments it is impossible to resist an extraordinary movement that
ecstatically carries oneself beyond oneself toward a feeling of intimacy
with everything.

I imagine a god who tenderly and passionately articulates the words
spoken by the father and repeated by the mother in *Ma Mère*: *"Put the
blame for everything on me."* (IV, 185) This is the god with whom
Nietzsche sought intimacy.

The convulsive distress of a child attends the night with an intimacy
that outstrips any formalized prayer. Reading the Biblical prophets, I
hear the screams of children, impotent refusals of what nonetheless
occurs.

Sacrifice

A Wave Overcoming a Wave. — I recall walking home one night, late autumn, frost, steam pouring out as I breathed; I was a bit drunk. Passing the woods, I heard a sudden outburst, one animal coming upon another. In the darkness I heard a furious struggle, a fight to the death. One of the animals, the one I figured was the predator, was fiercely shrieking; the other animal was grunting, breathing hard. I stood transfixed, all my attention concentrated through my ears. The struggle continued at the same level of intensity, a steady flame. Then suddenly there was change: the animal that had been shrieking began to whimper like a child. At that moment I realized I had mistaken the predator for the victim; and the sounds that had been so intense a moment ago were on the verge of stillness. The whimpering continued for awhile. The other animal, the predator, continued to make sounds similar to those he made earlier, only calmer, as if he was savoring the event. The victim fell into a silence from which he did not emerge, and this silence overwhelmed all other sounds.

Sacrifice is an extensive action, extremely charged, a scalding event. An animal's throat is slit, a cut into the night sea of the body; a shocking gush of blood streams and splashes out of pulsing darkness, accompanied by sacred and devastating tones.

A sacrifice is a transformation: it makes what is limited, infinite: what is useful, glorious; what is profane, divine. The sacrifice makes one dazzling, incomprehensible, writhing — emitting burning and blinding rays, a sun. One savors the moment of explosion, all explosions having a voluptuous character.

The skin breaks; the blood flows — the decisive unity of priest and victim.

Sacrifice renders the victim fascinating and appalling, beyond bounds. The victim exerts the allure of disintegration, the possibility of a boundless existence.

CƷ ᘏ

Sacrifice makes it blindingly clear: we are time, and time outstrips us.

CB ᘓᑎ

Extreme experience involves an abysmal experience of time.

CB ᘓᑎ

It is the thing — only the thing — that sacrifice wants to destroy in the victim. Sacrifice destroys an object's bonds of actual subordination, it uproots the victim from the world of utility and returns it to that of unintelligible caprice. (VII, 307)

Work, which subordinates objects (tools, animals) to humans, turns its objectifying force on humans as well. Humans themselves are mastered; they become things — farmers, factory workers, domestics. Assigned purposes, their significance is determined by their use. In the mundane world of work, humans exist in a servile state. An individual takes on the properties of the tools he or she controls, becoming regular, predictable, and manageable. Sacrifice interrupts the rhythm of work. At the moment of sacrifice, the victim explodes, and those who intently watch feel themselves become unstable, threatened, about to give way.

Sacrifice does away with the distinctions that are required for rational thought. Sacrifice destroys a thing's utility, which constitutes its intelligibility. What occurs does not make rational sense. Indeed there is a fundamental antagonism between rationality and sacrifice: the principle of rationality is preservation; the principle of sacrifice, destruction. The one is calm, productive, and purposeful; the other, wasteful, overwhelming, and immediate. In sacrifice the distinctions that kept things apart are dissolved, and the spectator enters into an intimacy unknown to rational thought. When the boundaries of the object are destroyed, the possibility of a subject-object split is also destroyed. Immanence is restored.

The return to immanent intimacy involves a clouded awareness. (VII, 308)

52

Rational consciousness is something other than immediate participation, and, so, it is not surprising that a dispassionate, rational mind would dismiss sacrifice as ridiculous or bizarre. Such designations notwithstanding, sacrifice has its own wild authority, its own intoxicating force.

ଓଃ ଡ଼ଠ

The chosen form of sacrifice varies from one religion to another. It may be something simple — some lemons, vermillion powder, or a few panicles of wheat — or it may take on a bloodier, more startling shape — a rooster, a goat, a bull, a child, and, at its height, even a God. In contemporary occidental culture, sacrifice is often purged of its gorier aspects, carried out in a purely symbolic fashion and given a theological significance. This attenuates the dramatic power of sacrifice (its terrifying, fascinating, unbearable aspects).

Theology tends to obscure rather than illuminate what occurs. Sacrifice is extreme, and theology, in an alliance with philosophy, is opposed to extreme experience. Theological dogmas attempt to establish limits and to articulate precise significance. In contrast, sacrifice obliterates limits and consumes significance; it draws one into an experience that disturbs any claim to certainty and assurance.

What is sacrifice no longer limited to symbolic significance, no longer wed to dogma? While this question may seem to ask for a definition of sacrifice, strictly speaking, sacrifice cannot be defined. It involves the dissolution of the boundaries that make definition possible. There is destruction, but it is not simple annihilation; for there is a release, and that which is set free is no longer determinate. Sacrifice means nothing. It is an incandescent destruction of meaning, a rupturing of limits, an epiphany of divinity. It sets loose a violence which surpasses and threatens to consume those who witness it. The visible and mundane disintegrate, and the sacred and terrifying appear. Time, which makes definitions impossible, erupts.

VanGogh's Ear, Shiva's Penis, Zeno's Tongue

— Did Jesus desire his crucifixion?
— Only in as much as he was a god.

Automutilation, perhaps the most shocking form of sacrifice, is, like all sacrifices, a violent act, revealing the sacred, the divine frenzy of time. To automutilate is to become divine, irreducible, a first unprincipled principle, an insubordinate event. The automutilator loses human blood but in doing so becomes divine, an immanent transcendence, an exorbitant event. The blood circles in the body, the time of the pulse, but when the body is torn open, the blood becomes an ecstatic explosion, gushing beyond limits; one pours out blood like the sun pours out rays, a tangential ejaculation, a sacred flow. The moment entails a rapt attention, like a lover diving from a cliff.

Automutilation emerges from a subterranean impulse. One tears one's flesh, cuts off an ear, or rips out an eye, and in doing so, willfully departs from standards, monstrously becoming the monster one is. The automutilator is priest and victim at once. The act transforms a human into a living sign of trespass, marking a departure from the order of conformity as surely as Prometheus' liver marks him a deviant among the gods. The automutilator defies integrity through a sovereign and ecstatic movement. Choosing to reject the standards in which others confine themselves, the automutilator undergoes a radical alteration, both the act and the result, transforming a human into something uncanny. A spurt of blood: a solar flare. A scar: sacred script.

CB 80

The tyrant Nicocrean experienced the scalding anarchy of automutilation: he was struck in the face by the solar explosion of a man who bit off and spit out his tongue; struck by the ferocious silence of a sovereign being who refused to speak in line with a tyrant's expectations.

CB

Music, myth, literature, and art are all sacrifices, wastes of words and effort, glorious nonsensical blazes.

CB 80

The reason one does not automutilate? Perhaps there is a servile inclination, a concern with being within the limits of the masters' desire,not to be something that would make their eyes pop out. Bataille's *Histoire de l'oeil* is a description of something blinding, something analogous to the opening scene of Bunuel's *Un chien Andalou*.

54

Abyss

Is not seeing seeing...?

Joy before death. — To be mortal is to be able to dance with death. When the dance ends, when I fuse, I will not be separate anymore; I will not be questionable anymore. I want to love being before death; being questionable is my only chance.

There is what I hesitate to call an intuition of the unknown. Absence too is evident. Approaching the night of night, one foot in chaos, I experience a reeling, hopeless levity.

> the flowers she brought still
> defiantly persisting
> a flower blown to points
> a precariously cresting wave

Cঙ ৪০

In *Ma Mère*, Lulu declares *"it is always pleasant to glide across a slippery surface."* (IV, 251) She could have added, "as long as one has the ability (or luck) not to fall." There is an undeniable intensity of experience when one is on the brink of falling, but to fall....

Each person gets as close as possible to the void, which is not to say very close, even, as far away as possible. But that which is dangerous for a timid soul may be delightful for someone of superabundant health. The more energy one has (the more lively one is) the more one is inclined to do things that less vital people regard as dangerously foolish, for example, Nietzsche calling the tables of value into question.

I am not just a being in a world; I am also a being in an abyss, a being that is by chance, a being that can, and eventually must, leave the world. I am connected to the world by my cares, but my dread connects me to....

— Where am I? Desperate, I pointed to the empty sky above. (III, 25)

I experience the emptiness of the sky as God, and it lends to everything its divinity. All oblations move toward it and are lost there, nowhere.

The immensity of the abyss indicates the improbability of my existence.

Born in the dark, dying against the dark, but a sun. The limits of logic are logically demonstrable, but that which is outside of logic, that which threatens and ruins calculation, is not. The unknown cannot be known, but it can be **experienced,** even felt to the point of terror. Here, theoretical insights are not essential — theoretical insights can only eclipse the shocking radiance of absence. Used perversely, logical explanation and argumentation can at best point toward the brink of absence, at which point they are ruined and abandoned.

During the night, knowledge and logic can only sedate what has to be felt. To assume what is not known is like the known, just not known yet, is to shirk an encounter with the radically unknown. The night, the night of nights, is not known, not the knowable. Reduced to the knowable, it poses no danger to what is known; that is, the disturbing character of the unknown is overlooked, as if the boundless is no threat to the bounded. We neglect how the unknown violates our capacity to know. Knowledge is always from the outside, requiring a subject-object relationship, the knower over and against the known. The most grandiose visions necessitate the most colossal steps beyond: Plato, standing outside of time; Hegel, outside of history. Such knowledge regards beings from the outside and is concerned with establishing and calibrating superficial limits. In contrast, inner experience attends to existence from within; it entails, not knowledge of the abyss, but being in the abyss.

CB ED

A different necessity. — When there is chance, nothing is necessary, and when nothing is necessary, it seems impossible to go on, and at some point necessary not to go on. Chance blossoms into necessity, the necessity of tragedy and ecstatic loss. All logical and rational foundations lacking, the abyss appears a nocturnal exigency, a dark torrent, one I cannot doubt, that bends my head back and cracks me open like a seed.

CB ED

56

Impossible

The extreme limit of the possible is impossible. Since Bataille strives for the unreachable, all his works are unfinished. Their incompleteness is not the result of a simple lack of energy or effort. While it is true that he lacked the strength to finish, it is also true that his works indicate an enormous struggle. The failure is not the result of weakness, but rather the limit of his strength. Such a collapse requires prodigious energies.

ᘓ ᘔ

My absurdity imagined, in a swoon, a means of exactly formulating the difficulty that literature finds. I imagined its object, perfect happiness, as a car that rushed along the road. I would pull up alongside this car on the left, at a dashing speed, without the hope of passing it. Then it accelerates some more and escapes me little by little, breaking away from me with the full force of its motor. Exactly at the very moment that it breaks away, my impotence to pass it is revealed, then following it, is the image of the object pursued by the writer: the object is only his on the condition that it is not grasped, but at the extreme limit of one's effort, it escapes terms with an impossible tension. At least, with the faster car's pulling away, I have experienced the pleasure, which at bottom would have escaped me, if it had not appeared to pass me that way. The more powerful car attains nothing, while the weaker car, which follows it, has an experience of the truth of pleasure, at the moment when the more rapid car gives him the feeling of recoiling. (III, 275)

> Eurydice drives away.
> Words come back to me.
>
> Writing involves impossible desires
> sands of silver and gold lost in dark ink
> the colors of the sun as it mingles with night.

It is at the apex of strength, when my energies are devoted to my desire, that the impossible smears everything I am or could hope to be.

Blood, sperm, shit, mucous galaxy. Diseases emanate from me like the waving barbs of an anemone.

> Eurydice gets away.
> Linos is with her.

Cʒ ᙏ

That which Bataille wrote about Emily Bronte, may also pertain to himself: *"She lived in a type of silence, the surface of which, only literature broke."* (IX, 173)

Literature attempts that which is unreachable, unknowable, and silent. It is a paradoxical and doomed effort: attempting to say what experience is, without abandoning a growing fidelity to its silence and inability to be known. It does violence to language, never content with what can be said, seeking instead what cannot be said, what perhaps should not be said. In contrast to work, which gets its value from what it achieves, literature achieves nothing if not failure. Like time, it is a movement of squander; like time, a waste of time; and like time, something glorious.

Like the fruit of time, a corpse, literature is dead, and being dead, it is dangerous.

Being inorganic, it is irresponsible. (IX, 182)

Literature lays claim to the endowment of religion, not its doctrines, but its mystical content. More specifically it is related to the rituals of sacrifice: both sacrifice and literature provide the opportunity to look at loss, even death, right in the face.

Our tragedies and comedies are the continuations of ancient sacrifices. (IX, 214)

Thus at the moment of the "mise à mort," they lean over their own nothingness. (VI, 45)

The fact that we are not adverse to loss, but rather to our inability to sustain loss, is indicated by the passion with which we desire stories in which the hero is subject to gross misfortune and danger. Because the events are fictional and our relationship to them is merely vicarious, we can endure them; we are free to be fascinated. Sacrifice and literature have a privileged (and duplicitous) status; they allow us to approach the dangerous with no real threat to ourselves.

Tragedy and comedy, and even the authentic novel, in the measure where they reflect, in the dazzling joy of their facets, the changing multiplicity of life, do they not respond as much as is possible to the desire for our ruin — tragically, comically — in the vast movement where we lose our being without end.
(VIII, 95)

Works of literature and art often attempt to increase the feeling of anxiety, seeking that which our rational behavior desires at all costs to avoid. As such, works of literature and art may reveal the depths of rationality, that is the depths from which rationality flees.

Cupid's Arrow

Eros is above all the tragic god. (X, 607)

If one lover says to another, "let's go die a little" we know what they intend to do.

Eroticism is akin to death. — They are both violent.
— Both are foreign to the order of things.
— We hide our sexual parts and we bury our dead.
— Both bring on intense emotion.
— Both render discourse mute.
— They involve shame.
— Great lovers frequently meet tragic fates.
— A young soldier before battle is as nervous as a virgin approaching a loved one.

Trembling: the only way of approaching the truth of eroticism... (X, 608)

Delay. — In *The Symposium*, Socrates claims to be an expert on erotics. Diotima, his teacher, from whom he learned about *eros*, is introduced as someone who has done great good: she caused a famine to be delayed. That is an odd thing: she did not prevent it, only delayed it. Diotima, the expert on erotics, is an expert at delay. Rationality, the calculative activity that is bent on survival, bent on avoiding whatever threatens, bent on not leaving things to chance, can, like Diotima, only, at best, delay. In the end, we cannot be rational; we cannot delay. The value of rationality, the value of delay is not in spite of the inevitable collapse, but because of it. If you are unaware of the inevitable collapse, you are incapable of intensely affirming and savoring the delay. It is the collapse that lends the time before the collapse its voluptuous character. Those who are oblivious of this tend to be sedate and insipid.

Socrates describes Eros as a daughter of Ingenuity: an ingenious way of dying?

When Nietzsche invites us to become the sea — a river losing itself in the sea — is he not inviting us to ecstasy, such as is found in erotic pursuits? The lover can become lost in the indeterminate immensity of the beloved's embrace.

Eroticism is not a simple return to animal sexuality: indeed, in comparison to human eroticism, animal sexuality appears to lack variety, and, so, indicates a compulsive restraint. The sexual activity of animals seems merely instinctive; they copulate when drive and opportunity coincide. Not so with us; we are not wholly driven by instincts. Rational behavior requires us to resist immediate desires, dedicating ourselves to anticipated results rather than immediate urges. Prohibitions play a central role in eroticism, or to be more precise, the breaking of prohibitions. With animals the sexual act does not involve the breaking of prohibitions; and so it lacks the wicked radiance it has for us. An animal cannot become animal, but, strangely, we can. When we slide toward erotic encounters, our divinity, like that of Zeus, involves a talent for turning animal.

Prohibitions encourage us to do that which will preserve us; eroticism answers the need we have for ruination. Consequently, eroticism and death are linked, two sides of the same process: the resurging proliferation of life. Furthermore, the extremes of sensuality involve an urge that resonates with death, an urge to surpass oneself, an urge to squander oneself. In eroticism uneasiness is desired; nothing is more enjoyable than being convulsively writhing.

Two lovers become the expanse between them. They become intimate with the tension that holds them apart.

ᴄᴈ ᴇᴏ

The total movement of life involves birth, sexuality, and death. In this view, death is the way that life gets out of its own way, making room for the resurgent movement that it is. Life would lose its vitality, its freshness, its charm, if it was not able to disregard that which had become exhausted. Life is an excessive expenditure, one that requires movement toward exhaustion: the desires that draw us toward exuberant excess, for example, our erotic tendencies, also draw us toward our

61

graves. Children take the places of those who bore them, getting on with the creative and destructive surge of life. In a comprehensive view of life, birth and death, proliferation and annihilation, renewal and decomposition require each other. To be able to spend — to live — is to be able to waste — to die. *Felix Culpa.*

CR

Mea Culpa

Forbidden fruit. — In the garden of Eden, there were many delicious fruits, fruits that one may suspect were just as tasty as the forbidden fruit. Therefore, it was not just the flavor, but the prohibition that made the fruit so irresistible. By being forbidden, it was transformed into an object of desire — the desire to transgress.

Identity. — When an individual transgresses the limits described by taboos, his or her identity is surpassed. This requires a divine energy.

Underground man. — The reason an individual is sent to prison and kept there is that he or she refuses to act the way a prisoner is expected to act; refuses to be passive, submissive, malleable. The crime that lands people in prison: not acting like a good prisoner.

༄ ༄

Hidden flaw. — We both obey and disobey laws; of all the animals we are the only ones who have such a relationship to laws. But when it comes to philosophical descriptions of humans, the fact that we break laws is ignored in favor of describing us as guardians and servants of the law; and so, we hide ourselves from ourselves.

Sinner's request. — *"Have pity on me! I have seen what you are."* (V, 63)

༄ ༄

A human is not allowed to sin; one must be a god for that.

༄ ༄

Can a transcendental ego sin? Can it breach its own integrity, communicate? Communication is a crime; it is daring to lean over the abyss.

"Communication" takes place only <u>between two beings</u> at risk — torn, suspended, and one and the other leaning over their nothingness. (VI, 45)

☙ ❧

Erotic passion, like mysticism, involves the obliteration of self. The anguish of intense eroticism is like the anguish of those who approach death. The loved one, escaping common limitations, is boundless, the occasion of becoming nothing. At the pinnacle of intensity, death becomes apparent, showing that the truth of love is death. The deepest love is onto death, and those who burn with it already feel this, this is the anguish of their love, the extraordinary price of their voluptuous being. If love is not capable of loving what is terrible about the other, it is an anemic passion, no more than a velleity; it is not love onto death. In extreme erotic encounters, one finds the other to be miraculous, incomprehensible, divine, the object of voluptuous worship. The claim that the truth of eroticism is death is not to contradict the assertion that eroticism centers on joy: both death and joy entail an ecstatic loss of the self, the one far more extreme than the other. Eroticism affirms being before breakdown, life in the face of death. Eroticism, like a festival, is a virulent denial of the primacy of one's future. What counts is now, taking on the being of a flame; but to be a flame is to fall toward darkness, tragically seduced by fathomless night. Light itself abandons everything that light ups. The truth of eroticism — of the night — is that a human being is not a thing.

What would I be without the night?

The value of eroticism. — If I had but a moment to live, I would want to live that moment as erotically as possible. If I could have what I want, I would have that which I could not bear. Delight like that would obliterate me.

Wounds

Compared to a slab of rock, a man or woman (or any other living being) is a wound, sensitive as a wound, lively as a wound, mortal as a wound.

Under the auspices of reason, pleasure is self-indulgence; but the extremes of pleasure are not self-indulging, but self-lacerating.

Whatever has the *experience* of being a surface, that is, of having an inside and an outside, is sovereign. At the extremes of a surface communication can occur, but only at the expense of the surface.

Tragic Affirmation

Does anything bring out our love of life as much as the proximity of death?

The extreme of joy — vertiginous intoxication — is found in the *approach* to the void. However, in order to experience joy, whether extreme or mild, it is necessary to be alive. Joy is not found in death, but in being before death. As much as we may enjoy being near the void — even without guard-rail — we do not want to fall in; quite the contrary, we want to go on expending, living gloriously.

Not zero, rather the approach is interminable. One lacks the energy to arrive at nothing.

It is in approaching death (being alive) that we find horror and delight. Death puts an end to our terror and laughter. Our love of being before death requires hostility toward death itself. That is why we must — if we love life — praise eroticism and condemn petty wars.

War and Eroticism

Our wars are a good measure of those impotent and reasonable professors who lead us. (VIII, 91)

That which we presently accept as war, militaristic war, is nihilism's most concrete manifestation. Nihilism is a hatred of life, an urgency to diminish and obliterate it. War goes too far, beyond being before death, beyond joy. War unleashes death, produces it, loves it, is it. Festival — eroticism — unleashes joy, the love of lingering, of being *before* death. Because we are communication, war is an attack on what we are.

The quest for political expediency and military solutions is the most dangerous problem we face today. Politics, as Levinas makes clear, is war. Consequently the truth of eroticism requires a defiance of politics, a detente of which politics is incapable, where wisdom is not a strategy for egology, but an encounter with what is beyond, requiring a generous expenditure of the energy that military men would reserve for the production of death.

We have amounts of energy at our command that we must dispense at any rate. (VII, 161)

We ought then lay down a principle from the fact that one day or another the amount of excess energy that we save up through work becomes so great that if the amount available for erotic ends is limited, it will be spent on a catastrophic war. (VIII, 162)

Aside from the lacuna implied by the order of utility, there is a more pressing dilemma: the problem of excess. If rational activity achieves its goal, it results in an excess. **This excess must be spent.** The dilemma is how: gloriously or catastrophically? The choice is between war, nihilistic and degrading, or eroticism, sumptuous and divine. In the end, the congruity of reason suggests the necessity of something incongruously unreasonable, delightful squander.

Descartes' thought demonstrates the need reasonable thought has for God, but reason's need for squander, which may also prove divine, is more insistent than the rational requirement for a supreme being.

The Agonal Character of Eroticism

What has passed for history is a history of war, that is, of nihilism. Eroticism has been neglected, deemed as insignificant. Struggle is not limited to war: life itself is struggle, and, for the healthy, a most enjoyable one. The contest that annihilates is war; the contest that invigorates is eroticism. There is a relation between *eros* and *agon*; indeed the relation is so close that it may be insightful to say that *eros* is *agon*. This relation prompted Nietzsche to describe love as an appreciation of having enemies. In love there is struggle; intercourse, whether verbal or corporeal, is a way of mixing it up.

ᛦ ᛤ

It is being before finale that lends the contest such fascinating magnificence.

ᛦ ᛤ

Fascination is mixed and made dense with horror. Leonardo da Vinci wrote of the repulsiveness of the sexual organs, but this repulsiveness is not the simple opposite of the desirable: in a more comprehensive view, that which is feared is also that which is desired. One fears something because it threatens to destroy, and, on occasion, one desires it because it promises disintegrating ecstasy.

ᛦ ᛤ

Lovers cannot count on each other, and that is what moves them to embrace so intimately as to be indistinguishable, lost together.

Breathing

We openly or secretly long for those occasions when we are on edge, acutely aware of our breathing, as if it were everything.

Extreme eroticism brings one to a sensation akin to that of someone who has been under water too long.

Lovers willingly seek the respiratory spasms a pulmonary victim avoids at all costs.

Although we may want to be breathless, we do not want to be utterly so.

Gasping for breath, almost on the verge of suffocation, one gains a feel for what one really is.

Mourning Song

Intonation:
let me be a man or a woman
let me not be an impostor

my spirit is the humor of my flesh
my soul is a hoax

The god speaks: It is life that is divine, and your life is your own.

Reading: Bonds must be broken if one is to be a free spirit. Science, beliefs, customs, ideas , traditions — these need to be put in the service of vitality. Spirit, God, Reason, History, and Soul — these ideas need to be broken. They distract from our lives — our endeavors and desires.

Credo

Not me.
I believe in nothing
especially not me.

I only believe that which I cannot help but see all around me — nothing.

In immediate experience there is neither God nor me.

Questions writhe into the absence of an answer.

C3 ››

I am not going to cram myself into some conceptual cage. I refuse to abdicate my sovereignty. I am not a servile dupe. I am next to nothing.

C3 ››

Experience is the authority to contest, and contestation is the method of experience. I am what it feels like to be, all descriptions of me — all words — are evasions. I refuse all designations. Contestation contests language.

C3 ››

Knowledge? There can be no knowledge of what I am! Knowledge not only falls short, it eclipses what I am: I am incomprehensible. When I ask what I am, I find no answer. I am a question without response.

71

When I ask what the universe is, I find no answer. I am lost. These questions are not theoretical; they are anxious.

CB   BO

To be is to be dramatic, and everything else seems evasion. Any configuration of myself from the outside, misses my being as communication; overlooks or degrades my dramatic capacity to decide. One has the authority to choose because one *is* dramatic.

Non Serviam

I am in no way distinguishable from god. For such a distinction I would have to be comprehended, and like god, intimate with his absence, I am incomprehensible.

Destruction indicates insubordination. Sacrifice reveals divinity.

☙ ❧

Contra ascetic impoverishment. — It is possible to reach the point of expenditure either through lack or excess. The ascetic chooses the former; Bataille, the latter. The ascetic does have experience — *feels* that he or she *is*; but does not reach the extreme limit; instead, only attains a paltry limit by ceasing to reach. Such a strategy insures the experience of loss by having so little to lose; there is *loss, but no great loss.* This is in contrast with extreme experience which seeks massive outpourings of strength. The limit is experienced through intense expenditure rather than impoverishment. Such failure is at the pinnacle of strength, like an explosive athlete experiencing the limits of speed. In asceticism one discovers one's limits and vulnerability by weakening oneself. The ascetic cuts off his legs in order to have the experience of being unable to catch up with the desired.

☙ ❧

Weakness versus strength. — The ascetic flees toward innervated states, abandoning life. A willful weakness brings on ecstasy, a voluptuous loss of self. But if one does not flee life, if one loves it, if one wants to live it to its extreme, then life itself becomes a radiant excess, an ecstatic event.

☙

At the extremes, silence rushes in on a wind.

La Gaya Scienze

The sovereignty of the free spirit. — The authority of experience is not the expertise of one who knows; it is the freedom of one who is lost in questioning, of one who must anxiously decide.

Divine nonsense. — The word 'sovereign' means nothing. It lacks sense like the word 'God' written by Meister Eckhart or Pseudo-Dionysius.

Uncertain freedom. — A free spirit seeks out uncertainty. Claims of certainty are signs of subordination, precluding the possibility of decision.

The chance of decision. — Indeterminacy is opportunity.

Sovereignty. — To be sovereign is to be unwilling to limit one's sense to servility. The moral good — thoroughly committed to the task of encouraging us to become tame workers (obedient slaves) — completely derides and dismisses the value of experience. Extreme health and its symptomatic laughter is always banished by moderate, moral men. Experience however is the sole value; everything else is dupery.

Free Spirit

Aware of the abyss, Nietzsche is the herald of the night, singing the lonely night song. His thought takes place at a decisive moment, when the belief in devitalizing values has reached its exhaustion, when all the great doctrines and teachings appear to be crumbling, on the verge of disintegrating into the abyss. The foundation lacking, Nietzsche's winged thought rises without ground, and at the crest of his thought are his majestic teachings, each of them defiantly cast against an abyss. In this boundless and bewildering expanse, any and every idea can be refuted. This experience is the chance to become aware that the value of existence is not found in any knowledge, dogma, or idea; it is found in life itself. Nietzsche is the herald of the abyss; he is also a friend of humankind.

The destiny of humanity has encountered pity, morality, and the most opposing attitudes: anguish or, even more often, horror: it has hardly encountered friendship. Until Nietzsche. (V, 284)

Friendship, the opposite of pity, spares the friend nothing difficult, challenges the friend to be a man or a woman. As a friend of mankind, Nietzsche gives us a gift: an awareness of the abyss, a sensibility that may spur a man or a woman to be to become something more. Nietzsche envisions a being that looks down on humans like humans look down on apes. The designation "human being" is not a spur, it is a trap — an obstacle for one who would go beyond.

cs 80

If we were to represent Nietzsche and Bataille as isolated individuals we would limit them with the concept 'man'.

cs 80

Liberal Education? — The education one receives at a university often indicates nothing more than an aptitude for conforming to the powers that control, determine, and govern universities. The habits of intelligence inculcated are, for the most part, habits of subservience.

Identity of oppression. — My identity is a linguistic construction that misses what I am.

"Know thyself." — The Delphic inscription is an insidious seduction, a call to chains. What I am cannot be known.

"Become who you are." — In order to take up the Pindaric challenge, it is necessary to die to yourself. In truth you are something other than yourself, something other than what is known. *Ecce Homo* is a record of such a death and birth.

Slaves that have become masters. — Science, industry, ideology, institutions, political organizations, laws.

Entrance requirements. — Faith requires a capacity for the insipid and domineering.

Dazed. — People persistently make statements so inane that in order to make them at all it is necessary for them not to take their lives seriously, assuming either that their lives will go on forever or that this life is just some kind of preliminary exercise.

Boring lives. — Boring lies. Certain fictions invigorate more that others.

Tradition. — It is not customary to consider customs as merely customary, unless, of course, they are strange customs, in which case it is customary to dismiss them as being nothing but customs.

Strange authority. — It is Nietzsche's acquaintance with the abyss that grants him the right to scoff at "big words".

A noble education. — An education should teach the importance of defiant indeterminacy, and provide a hard schooling in refusing all designations.

The hard school. — There is a range of cruelty that spiritually anemic souls, having a poor perspective, fail to see. They see all cruelty to be essentially like their own, that is, cruelty out of resentment, the kind of cruelty that is systematically inflicted by penal justice systems. What they fail to see is that there is another cruelty, one that comes from abysmal heights, the cruelty of the noble spirit. Noble people, noble tribes, often have extremely painful rites of passage. They inflict pain as a gift, the greatest gift possible. No one comes of age — becomes a lover of struggle, a lover of tragedy, a lover of life — without pain. Because of this, noble education involves pain, but pain as a gift, one that gives the sufferers a feel for who they are.

 C3 80

A frightened child can be told a story to relieve fear. But to come of age is to see these stories for what they are — comforts for children. And the tale of a life is something other than a story for a child. The end is always the same, and it is not happy. To be an individual is not to take one's place in relation to someone's story or dogma; it is to be what one is.

C3 80

There is a need for revelation, but that does not imply that there is revelation, no more than starvation indicates that there is food.

C3 80

You are nothing without pain. (V, 310)

Music lesson. — A friend once told me that immediately after experiencing the greatest pain in her life she was able to play the piano in a way that she had never been able to previously or since.

In certain street gangs if a member violates the gang's code, he is beaten from head to toe for a specified period of time, which is determined by the severity of the violation. At the end of the beating, the gang members embrace the victim. When one has been wounded, one gains a sensitivity for things that those who have not suffered cannot appreciate.

Doestoevsky's underground man claims that pain is more valuable than mathematics. Without a painful education (an education that is inevitable though sometimes it comes too suddenly, too late, or too violently) an individual is oblivious to communication — how things feel. Suffering sharpens consciousness, makes us sensitive to tragedy and loss. It brings us closer to our existence. Mathematics, in contrast blunts dramatic being, sedates us. Since pain occurs at the limits of calculation, where calculation fails, it teaches the limits of reason; it introduces the unreasonable, uncertain, unstable, and incomprehensible. Since it is pain, it does so in the most intimate manner. We find ourselves becoming unreasonable, uncertain, unstable, incomprehensible. This anxious instability is our freedom. Who has not been stung by his or her wildness? Frightened by what he or she is?

Nietzsche As Educator

To have a master like Nietzsche is to no longer believe in masters; it is to be familiar (even intimate) with nothing. One is abruptly set free — painfully, dangerously free. It is to be confronted with the anxious task of creation.

All causes should lead like a poem to an absence of causes. The joy of life, its deepest nonsense, is not found in serving a cause.

Lessons on Perspective. — 1) There are a plurality of perspectives. 2) Certain perspectives are more interesting — more rare — than others.

Bataille has an extreme perspective, exquisitely rare: that of a sick man in the middle of a war zone. In the middle of an invading abyss, he is almost nowhere.

Nietzsche's revaluation of values is time itself, tragedy itself. Those who cannot bear the truth of time and tragedy are driven to avoid it. Nietzsche himself described his revaluation as a war, and a war, perhaps more than any other event requires rapt attention; and so, unless we have an ardent awareness, we will not appreciate Nietzsche's wager.

Morality stinks. — Morality is like cosmetic hygiene, attending to life from the outside in; but vitality is from the inside out.

Ubermensch. — Nietzsche suggests something forbidden so far: a sovereign being who finds life beguiling. For Nietzsche it is not a question of man, but of the body. The body is to be intensified, which requires an overcoming of man.

What the word 'Nietzsche' invokes: An awareness of the void versus a nostalgia for lost worlds. This is the contrast between freedom (always linked to tragedy and the abyss) and servitude (anything that defines and thus limits, whether it be a Fatherland, a theological doctrine, or a world of the forms — all attempts to stifle the exuberance of time, attempts to keep us within prescribed boundaries).

Bataille writes about Nietzsche the way a friend would, the way a lover would.

CB ED

Work is not enough. Work should be the slave of health. If work does not intensify health, what good is it? At the extremes of health, health itself becomes generous, needs to radiate itself.

The task (it is still a task) is not to get rid of reason (work), but to use work to achieve radiant intensity, using project to get beyond project, words to get beyond words. It is a task to get out of work, a wicked one from the perspective of those who would have us consumed by work. We want to be consumed by joy.

Work takes place in paradoxical time, "putting off existence until later," and if one does nothing but work, one never gets around to living. Both "joy," Nietzsche's word, and "glory," Bataille's word, indicate a radiant state which is valuable in itself, where life is not put off. Joy is life. One might say that joy is the meaning of life, its highest sense, but that would be misleading, for in fact joy is nonsense. Nonsense is the pinnacle of sense.

CB ED

The sciences, having only a practical significance, should be subordinate to our life. They should be used; instead they have been given a sovereign position in relation to us: we are used by science; science dictates our ends. Science is worthy only to the extent that it makes people more intense, more alive, more joyous. Unfortunately, its dominant effect is now to make people more sterile, more flat-headed, more useful clay.

Challenge: Take delight in this — you are not dead yet.

CB ED

In the water, but beneath me, like words, is the sea floor. I swim out over the reef, and looking down, I see the depths becoming more and more strange. Then, past the reef, no ground. My heart dilates. I float like a fetus or a star.

ʊ ʒ

I know what someone who knows nothing knows. Quietly, I spill into silence...

It is difficult not to confuse life with its shells — grammar, politics, economies, cultures, architecture, moral systems.

ʊ ʒ

I refuse all moral collars and conceptual leashes. For the most part I do not bother to deconstruct, I let indifference break my bonds. Where there is no love... I want to take heed of what words miss. I take special care not to mistake useful abstractions for reality.

ʊ ʒ

At the extremes of health, I go beyond what I have been, ecstatic. I want more energy than I need. I want to feel it; be it. I want explosive strength, the energy to overcome constraints. I want to be dangerously healthy, more healthy than is permitted, more healthy than is prudent.

Health is an extreme state, an excess; when one has it, one is innocent, careless. The more intense one is, the more there is a love of adventure, a love of going at things with no idea of what is going to happen. The unknown appears laden with charm.

When Nietzsche calls for the value of selfishness, he does not mean an augmentation of the ego. The self is not an ego; it is the body. Furthermore an intensified self is more prone to generosity, sensitivity, and mercy than its pathetic, devitalized, dutiful counterpart.

Nietzsche's philosophy is a quest for health, hitherto unimaginable vitality. No longer a man, he became an explosive charge, a sun.

81

Felix Culpa

I do not want to be perfect.
Felix Culpa.
I do not want to be immortal.
Mea Culpa.
I want to live.
Felix Culpa.

There are people who are inclined to sum up Bataille's thought as nihilism. (They would indite Nietzsche on similar charges.) I imagine they would find the following quote to be useful in constructing their arguments.

To imagine oneself, the self rubbed out, abolished by death, that the universe would lack... Completely to the contrary, if I would subsist, with me a mob of other cadavers, the universe would age, all these corpses would give it a bad taste. I am able to bear the weight of the future only on one condition: that others, always others, live there — and that death washes us away, then washes these others away without end. (V, 33)

They fail to see that Bataille's statements are symptomatic of a position directly opposed to nihilism. By affirming the movement toward death, Bataille is affirming life. Life is that which is over and against death. If there was no death, we would not have the lives that we do. To affirm mortality is to affirm life, and to imagine life as something other than finite is to choose a distracting fantasy. Life is defiance of death, for without its rhythmic lover and enemy, it would lose its agonal and glorious character. There is no glory without death; there is no light without darkness. Our being is in burning.

Affirmation of existence. — If you cannot affirm incompleteness and imperfection, you cannot affirm that which you *are*. To be a lover of what we are, it is necessary to love all tragedies real and imagined. **Those who neglect to affirm tragedy, they are the nihilists; they do not love what is. They hate time; they attempt to avoid it.**

Love of the enemy. — If one has enough strength, there is a need to defy death, consequently, a need for death.

Tragedy is the extreme of comedy, comedy that cannot endure.

The Scream of the Dying

The scream of the dying man is not a proclamation of death; it is an affirmation of life. It is not death that screams, but life in the face of death, a futile and doomed declaration of sovereignty, a tragic defiance. The scream is the sound of a being attempting to be, struggling, existing all at once, holding nothing back, life reaching a high point of intensity, ecstasy.

 C3 8O

Death an elixir. — You will not be there for your own death, and so, in this sense, it is not really your own. It will be for others to attend. If you love those who will gaze upon your corpse, perhaps the most you can hope is that when they will look upon it they will be delighted to still be alive and that your death will be an elixir for the living, silently exhorting them not to take life for granted. Death, as Nietzsche wrote, should be for the living, an occasion for festivals, and your death, a festival you cannot attend. When you die, death will steal your awareness of dying. You will not even hear the music. You will not be dancing with death; you will be lost in her embrace.

I die to the extent that I am aware of dying. But death steals awareness, I am not simply aware of dying; death is simultaneously stealing this awareness from me .... (V, 241)

C3 8O

Depraved loss. — The awareness that a being is irreplaceable is most acute when it is about to be lost. It is miserable when the sovereign nature of life is not apparent until the end.

C3 8O

Some critics of Anselm's arguments claim that being is not a predicate: one cannot **be** more than another; being is being. These critics carry the principle of identity too far, mistaking their useful techniques for ontological insights. Once we put aside the homogeneous assumptions inherent in logic, a heterological arrangement asserts itself: not all beings equally are. Not only do certain beings exist more intensely than others (for example a falcon versus a sponge), but also an individual may be more intense at one time than at another (sometimes fervent, sometimes exhausted). When Bataille writes, *"MEN ACT IN ORDER TO BE,"* (I, 433) it cannot be understood without a heterological appreciation of being, without an appreciation for the fact that certain beings, sovereign beings, **are** more than others, and that other men, masters, deprive others, the servile, of their very being. When a human is a tool, his or her very being has been diminished.

CŽ ŽO

Masters, for the most part, are servile, dependant leaches. That is not what I mean by sovereign. Nor do I mean: your choice of Caesars.

CŽ ŽO

Humans, like electrons, are only tentatively held in orbit around various principles. Their relative autonomy, which is always maintained, even in the most demanding orbits, allows for the possibility of calling everything into question. While the orbit allows an individual to make sense, providing the illusion of being a satellite around a stable sun, nonetheless there persists the possibility of being exorbitant, of being a sun oneself.

The bonds that hold molecules together are chemical; the bonds that hold planets in their orbits are gravitational; and the bonds that hold humans to their various centers — ideas, institutions, governments — are often no more than words.

CŽ ŽO

That for which life strives, that which makes life valuable in itself, is its intensity. Intensity is sovereignty. It is too much. Being at the extreme is uncertainty, which is manifested not through an open calculation, but through a boundless current of dread. At the extremes being is nowhere.

Light itself is blind.

ଔ ଊ

The Banquet of Prometheus

Prometheus stealing divine fire. — I will put it bluntly: Prometheus liked having his liver eaten daily. Like the Christian Eucharist, it is a banquet characteristic of superabundant divinity. He found great joy in having his liver devoured by vultures — in experiencing himself as divine and insubordinate flesh. The daily sacrifice was a sign of his genuine divinity, for through his sovereign crime — his irrational gift and theft — he refused to obey even the laws of the gods. Like a solar flare out of the sun, he went crashing beyond the limits that constrained other gods, becoming even more divine. In comparison to him, the other gods are tame; even Zeus is predictable, with his thunderbolt prop, guiding all things like a rational principle. Prometheus' fiery disobedience broke the ring of selfish calculation; he became ecstatic glory.

ॐ

Spare me any abstract rubbish! What is freedom without exhilaration? You are not free to decide; you are free if you decide. It is not given; it is taken. Everything else is verbiage; faith is a confidence game.

ॐ ॐ

They show me a thoroughly tame creature, one completely subordinated to and legitimated by institutions, and they expect me to take that pathetic weakling — that good boy — for an ideal? Forget it! *"Facing decadence, I no longer see an ideal."* (VI, 73)

ॐ ॐ

With increased health comes an increased desire for danger, but also an increased ability to get away with it, which is not to be confused with security.

Saturnalia

Looking for the light, we found a blinding thing, indistinguishable from night; and seeking the night there too we found a sun.

෨

You encouraged us to seek the truth, and we desperately sought it, but found only the search itself, our despair, and this: all truths are lies.

Our desire for truth opens the door beyond words, where truth is nowhere.

We are lost, but being full of daring, we are enchanted.

෪ ෩

Extreme affirmation. — The extremes of Bataille's joyous affirmation: he imagines a man laughing himself to death.

Everyone is conscious that life is parodic and that it lacks an interpretation. (I, 81)

Since being is time, ontology is the occasion of laughter. If you are not able to laugh at something, for example yourself, you have not yet achieved the truth. In short, you are still capable of being impressed, able to be suckered by illusions of renown and prestige, unable to glimpse with a mocking eye how laughably groundless everything is. To be mirthless is to be unable to see the centerless centrality of parody, each pretension of preeminence mocked to its absent core by its other. At the extremes of laughter there is no reason to laugh, but everything becomes laughable.

෪ ෩

Paradoxical Thought

"Being is nowhere." — Where else could it be?

Nothing extreme. — At the extreme of prayer, there is no prayer. At the extreme of poetry, there is no poem.

Overwhelming nonsense. — Science is incapable of dealing with nonsense, and, consequently, it has a paucity of sense, being limited to what is merely useful.

Question. — If you never wonder what it is to be a man or a woman how could you ever expect to be one?

Doestoevsky wrote that if there is no god, anything is possible. **Anything** is possible, even, as Nietzsche wrote, gods, that is, extreme states.

The instability of the copula. — The verb to be can be anything. The verb being is unstable, the unstable basis which is not a basis, which binds things together in a moment during which they are lost.

The absence of god does not clear the way for this or that abiding center, rather anything, which in time can be replaced by anything else. The death of God unleashes the impossibility of abiding, time itself in all its otherness, washing over us.

> *A desire to rise is a desire to fall.*
> The way up and the way down are the same.

> *Incipit tragoedia.*
> *Incipit parodia.*

Abbé C.

A libertine is a parody of a saint, and, of course, vice verse, completing a circuit of dread and desire, piety and scandal, sobriety and intoxication. *L' Abbé C.* is full of parodies. Robert is described as a parody of his twin brother Charles:

Robert fascinated me: he was the comic double of Charles: Charles gutted, under the disguise of a cassock. (III, 241)

He is also a dejected double of the editor:

I was frightened of resembling that fascinating but pitiable man. (III, 241)

There are many other parodies. Charles' sarcasm is a parody of the truth, and the truth, in turn, a parody of his sarcasm, the truth being an overly solemn double, a derisive lie, and being all the more laughable — and dreadful — because of its somber attitude.

The chasm that separates Charles and Robert is their similarity: Robert's principles are as empty as Charles' lack of principles. An ecclesiastic's principles are a sham double of a licentious man's emptiness.

So it was the similarity, not the opposition of our characters, that has led us to display inconsistent feelings, that were most likely to deceive and irritate the other. (III, 291)

This absolute opposition had the sense of a perfect identity. (III, 291)

This perfect identity, however, is not really an identity understood as something that can be precisely defined. It is rather a common indeterminacy, an empty and undefinable existence that is manifest in anxiety. The parodic difference between Robert and Charles is what they have in common, their sameness — a common instability — gives rise to difference; they are driven by their common indeterminacy toward opposing commitments (to which, ironically, they are never wholly committed.) *"A changing irony had lead him to piety."* (III, 291)

The difference between Robert and Charles is due to Robert's choice of masks, a cleric's cassock.

The capacity — and need — to act, to mask themselves, is linked to the depths of the abyss that joins them.

I do not limit my being to what I know. Being intimate with the unknown, I myself am unknown. I am a body. Tangible and strange. Words come out of me like clouds out of the sea. Do not mistake the clouds for the sea. My body is a river and a circuitous sea.

CŽ ßŊ

Deadly Decision. — Decision is other than project: it is being all at once, holding nothing back. In despair, after one dies to oneself, one can give birth to oneself, but in doing so one only gives birth to a creature already dying.

Decision is the play — the trembling — of chance.

Raw

What does it feel like to be you? What is your tone, tempo, and intensity? The raw event of existence — feel this and refuse all designations!

CB ❧

By means of language and work, I preserve myself, but if I limit myself to that, I avoid what I am. Language and work, sharing the same temporality, involve me in a world of anticipation; I become concerned with what is not yet; absorbed by something other than immediate existence, inattentive to how it feels to be.

Stripped of interpretation and purpose, no longer identifying myself, I am only how I feel. This cannot be articulated; nevertheless, it is sometimes possible to hear it in someone's voice — how it feels to be. It is profoundly communicated when words fall apart.

CB ❧

There is no hiding it. One's choice of masks — like a child on Halloween — only serves to give one away.

Concealing is so revealing.

CB ❧

Silence is the holy of holies; no words may enter there.

CB

Fragments of a Philosophical Work

A child's rag. — It is not intelligence that makes someone reach and grasp for reasonable beliefs and other scraps of rhetoric.

All too human. — To be human: not to acknowledge that you are an animal, and to prefer familiar lies to immediate experience.

Fire! — It is one thing to think about passion and it is another to catch fire. Socrates thinks; Alcibiades burns. Heidegger thinks; Bataille burns.

Phenomenology. — For Husserl the whole of experience is considered fodder for the formal. Phenomenology is the negation of experience. Experience overflows knowledge; they are only wed if experience is kept within useful and reasonable limits. Phenomenology, with its reductions and *epoche*, feigns to break with all dogmatic paradigms, but when it makes this announcement, it gets down on one knee before language and two knees before knowledge. Once doctrines have fallen into the analytic divisions which often characterize criticism, there is a renouncement of fusion — a renouncement of *"the only form of intense life."* (V, 22) Even when it characterizes itself as philosophy of experience, philosophy is oblivious to the extremes of experience.

Dissolution of the subject. — Just as I do not know ecstasy, I do not experience it. The I is a correlate of knowledge, an ego, Husserl's subject pole; ecstasy, in contrast, contests, even negates, the I. It is not the subject that contests; it is the subject that is contested. It is not the I that experiences; rather the I is ecstatically ruptured and dissolved in experience.

Husserl's abyss. — Apodictic certainty is a doxic modality.

Philosophical move. — At the extreme limit, where a boundless and threatening perplexity begins, philosophy interjects a metaphysical given, a solid basis. All philosophers seem to do this, differing from one another only in what they assume the basis to be.

Pragmatic solutions. — If a question can be solved, it can be given a pragmatic answer. Do not get carried away by this claim, for the truly momentous questions demand decision, not solutions.

Religion and Reason. — Religion within the bounds of reason alone is devoid of the sacred.

CB EO

Rigorously hollow. — As if being systematic and rigorous makes one less pretentiously inflated; all it does is puff one up in a systematic and rigorous manner, which is to say thoroughly.

Questions for answers. — What turns people into the blinking dolts Nietzsche described? They are afraid of being what they are, afraid of being infinite, ignorant supplication.

Reciprocity. — There are two types of people who speak in accord with revelation: 1) the fake, that is those who pretend to have ultimate knowledge, and 2) the gullible, that is those who place their confidence in the pretentious.

Confident con artists. — If a confidence game is to be truly efficient, it must take in those ones who carry it out, sincere priests and earnest psychoanalysts.

Close reading. — It is possible to read philosophers not as insights into the universal nature of existence, but rather as bizarre accounts of interesting and strange men, stories of individuals who carried on monologues that claimed to speak for everyone, only slightly tarnished by the fact that they could not be sure that other people exist.

Scientific ventriloquism. — Reason kills God, then imitates his voice, but why kill God if you still want the stable authority and sedate comfort the illusion provided?

Absence. — The absolute context is absent. This absence is the possibility of positing a wide array of absolutes, and it is the possibility of dismantling any absolute.

Kant. — Kant woke from his dogmatic slumbers in order to take a more effective sleeping pill: transcendental idealism.

Certain bet. — What revelation feigns to have revealed—the origin and the end, the past and the future — are not known. One can only hazard a guess. Revelation is the pretense of a safe bet, a sure thing, a life without risk.

Tools

Knowledge. — Stated simply: knowledge is a tool; it concerns what is useful. Existence however is divine. What makes life worth living is not simply that which allows us to remain alive, but that which makes it glorious. Of course, it is necessary to be alive in order to be glorious, thus the value of knowledge, a secondary and subordinate value.

Perspective. — The useful being regards the entire universe in his or her own image, i.e., as something useful.

What is knowledge purged of beliefs? — A set of wrenches, a plumb line, an instruction manual, but for what?

Abysmal backdrop. — My existence, your existence, came to be, and continues to be against all possibility.

The Fool's Heart

Very bright. — There is a fear of the night that compels people to avoid the night; the result is the certitude of an individual who goes to sleep early and rises with the sun and declares: "there is no night."

A good joke. — A man appears most ridiculous when he refuses to admit how foolish he is — when he, himself, is a joke that he tries desperately not to get.

CR

The fool said in his heart, 'there is no God,' but a foolish thought pushed to its extreme is not laughable; it is terrible. A foolish thought is a terrible one that can be avoided for now.

What I am afraid of is going to happen.

When pain is no longer before pleasure, it is agony, not delight.

Tragic Verse

Out of the blue. — Mahler wrote the last movement of his sixth symphony, which describes "three blows of fate, the last of which fells him like a tree", during one of the most happy and serene periods of his life.

Apex. — Things are surpassed at their height.

The divine tragedy. — The tragic is divine or at least the occasion of the divine: it can make a human call out to God.

Anxious exhaustion. — It is impossible to maintain sovereign existence; it squanders the energy needed to maintain it. The sun exhausts itself.

 CB 80

Sacrifice is the perverse project of dissolving project, of rendering what was useful and determined (indeed determined by its utility) useless and indeterminate. The useful can be sacrificed by destroying its utility. For some beings this entails a knife and flame, but there are other means, ways that result in incandescence without taking the path of fire. Poetry is a sacrifice in which words lose their utility. Poetry does not work; it dazzles.

Bataille's writings are a place of sacrifice. Philosophy, History, and Reason are its victims. While common language is effective, useful, and efficient, Bataille's work is none of these. Instead, it interrupts work — strange words which do not get a grip on anything. The lines of ink that mark his pages do not indicate forms and limits; they are cracks, similar to the slits opened up by a sacrificial priest. What appears in the cracks is a profound lack of sense, a vertiginous abyss.

The horror of being God.

The texts are often fragmented, punctuated by voids of silence where words are wasted. The most profound aspect of *La Somme Athéologique* is a silent, desperate absence.

His prayers reach out, but they cannot grasp. Whether written or spoken, they are a waste of breath. They are written or said when nothing else can be, when there is nothing to do.

Cʒ ꙭ

The sacrifice of god does not make sense; it is the most catastrophic unfolding of nonsense. It indicates a tragic movement that is incomprehensibly pervasive. Eli lamma sabachtani.

Cʒ ꙭ

Decision is "once and for all." As such it has the temporality of God.

Cʒ ꙭ

Out of the depths, out of the depths — an abysmal energy, overwhelming, a force that is all at once.

Cʒ ꙭ

In a state of extreme supplication, out of necessity one may cry out to God, but now the word "God" is an admission of one's inability to comprehend God.

Cʒ ꙭ

The "Lamma sabachtani" is a revelation of incompleteness, a revelation of the absence of revelation. Prayer is supplication; everything else is flattery, bargaining, and posing.

☙ ❧

The abyss shreds Bataille's thought, leaving it in fragments. Nietzsche was aware of the abyss, his aphoristic and poetic texts often bear its uncanny mark.

☙ ❧

The mundane world is whatever can be grasped and comprehended; it is what it is for humans. The sacred however outstrips human comprehension, and yet it is encountered. It is unavoidable.

☙ ❧

Dianus

In the Introduction to *Le Coupable*, Bataille uses the pseudonym Dianus, writing: *"One named Dianus wrote these notes and died."* (V, 239) In a grove at Nemmi, there grew a sacred oak, guarded by a priest. The grove and particularly the oak was sacred to Diana, the huntress. Her priest was called Dianus, King of the Wood. In order to become Dianus it was necessary to become thoroughly intimate with sacrifice. More precisely, it was necessary to attack and kill the one who presently held the office.

During this furious ordination, there was a moment when both the murderer and the victim shared the same existence, both lost in priestly violence. Dianus killed in order to become the next victim. The sacrifice which perpetuated this priesthood engendered a profound compassion, a deep complicity with the void; and, once attained, this priesthood must have carried with it an incomparable intensity of experience, a relentless defense against complacency, a ferocious attentiveness to time. Dianus sought vulnerability. To embrace this fate was to affirm being in a desperate situation. It was to seek fear itself, to strive to be what one cannot help but be — mortal. To will to be Dianus was to will to be tragic, fleeting, sacred.

ℭℜ

At the beginning of *The Golden Bough*, Frazer claims that the rule of this priesthood had no parallel in antiquity, but he overlooks an ever insistent candidate, time. Like the King of the Wood, each moment is attacked where it stands. This priesthood consecrated time and those who want to be time; but time is other, even other than itself; and in time, time washes over itself. Each moment a violent outbreak and a yielding victim.

ℭℜ

Language typically dodges the mortal fate that Dianus desired; avoids the thought that we too are time. Preoccupied by survival, rational truths are denials of the violent and fragile blossoming of time. Among words, only poetry attempts to take heed of it, but when the moment comes, all men, like poets and priests, are compelled to attend; still at the extreme of poetry, at the extreme of prayer, poems and prayers give out....

101

Monody

Fuliginous, fiery and ashen emotions amid a deafening roar. A river of canary and coral flame bending, writhing, twisting beyond itself, urgently insisting that it not be as it is now. All this amid a valley of midnight blue, coursing down from a mountain, sparking lemon against Bengal rose. Deeper, deeper than violet mired in burnt umber, eye-crushing black, folding into the night of nights.

> ...vividly alive
> leaning over a tomb
> grateful to ...

ఆ ಬ

Purple, crimson, dark violent thought, a thousand hearses could not carry you away.

To read Bataille is to have a feel for what it is like to be dealt a mortal wound, or, more precisely, to be struck in an already mortal wound.

ಆ

> All is fire and water and drifting air.
> The earth itself gives way.
>
> To be is to be on the verge of not to be.
>
> I am king of the wood.
> Silence rushes in on a wind.